Praise for the novels of Cassie Edwards

"High adventure and a surprise season this Indian romance." —*Affaire de Coeur*

"Edwards puts an emphasis on placing authentic customs and language in each book. Her Indian books have generated much interest throughout the country, and elsewhere." —*Journal-Gazette* (Mattoon, IL)

"Few can relate a story as well as Ms. Edwards." —*Midwest Book Review*

"Edwards consistently gives the reader a strong love story, rich in Indian lore, filled with passion and memorable characters." —*Romantic Times*

"Excellent . . . an endearing story . . . filled with heartwarming characters." —Under the Covers

"A fine writer . . . accurate. . . . Indian history and language keep readers interested." —*Tribune* (Greeley, CO)

"Captivating . . . heartwarming . . . beautiful . . . a winner." —*Rendezvous*

"Edwards moves readers with love and compassion." —*Bell, Book & Candle*

Also by Cassie Edwards

WIND WALKER

Cassie Edwards

A SIGNET BOOK

SIGNET
Published by New American Library, a division of
Penguin Group (USA) Inc., 375 Hudson Street,
New York, New York 10014, U.S.A.
Penguin Books Ltd, 80 Strand,
London WC2R 0RL, England
Penguin Books Australia Ltd, 250 Camberwell Road,
Camberwell, Victoria 3124, Australia
Penguin Books Canada Ltd, 10 Alcorn Avenue,
Toronto, Ontario, Canada M4V 3B2
Penguin Books (N.Z.) Ltd, Cnr Rosedale and Airborne Roads,
Albany, Auckland 1310, New Zealand

Penguin Books Ltd Registered Offices:
80 Strand, London WC2R 0RL, England

First published by Signet, an imprint of New American Library,
a division of Penguin Group (USA) Inc.

First Printing, June 2004
10   9   8   7   6   5   4   3   2   1

I dedicate *Wind Walker* to my sweet nephew
Andy Raymer of Texas and his lovely wife, Cathy.
Love,
Aunt Cassie

A Warrior's Dream

She glides over mountain, hills, and stream,
Crying her song into the Warrior's Dream.
She tells of things he does not want to hear,
She cries a sorrowful and painful tear.
No longer free to glide in tomorrow's skies.
She bows her head into the wind and cries.
If only for a moment,
Forever in his dreams,
They bow their heads together,
And into the wind—
       they scream.

Belinda Villanueva, poet and friend

Chapter 1

I had no time to hate, because
The grave would hinder me,
And life was not so ample I
Could finish enmity.
                    —Emily Dickinson

THE WYOMING TERRITORY, 1868

Smoke spiraled slowly upward from the central lodge fire, escaping through the smoke hole overhead. A long-stemmed pipe lay on one of the round stones that circled the fire, the tobacco in the bowl only ash.

The pipe had been shared by the warriors of the Golden Eagle Clan of *Sha-hiyena*, Cheyenne, who sat around the fire, attentive to the proud, young warrior Wind Walker.

"My brethren, our scouts have brought word to us that another wagon train of white eyes passes not far from our village." Wind Walker sat with his legs crossed, his back straight. His gaze moved from man to man as he spoke to them in an authoritative voice. "Our scouts also saw more signs of Ute renegades. These renegades have no morals, no souls. They raid wagon trains and ambush tribes that ally themselves with us Cheyenne."

Wind Walker stood and went to the entryway of the huge conical-shaped council house. He looked at his people peacefully doing their daily chores. His heart warmed at the sight of the children playing. They were so innocent.

As a man of peace, he had vowed long ago to do everything within his power to keep the children safe. They would grow into vital, strong adults who would protect the Cheyenne. The children were the future of his people, whether it survived or faded away. Wind Walker prayed often to *Maheo*, who created the world, people, and all animals and birds of the earth, to watch over and protect them.

Had his wife not died, by now he might have a child of his own to watch and admire.

He ached for a child. Yet Wind Walker had not found a woman who compared with his Sweet Willow, whom he had loved with all his heart. Thankfully, he could sleep now each night without dreaming of her. He had finally accepted her death and felt ready to move on.

In time, his life would be filled with a

woman he could call his own and their children.

But now he had other things to do. A lot rested on Wind Walker's shoulders, and he would not let anyone down.

He turned to the warriors. "My brethren, I would like to go and speak with the head man at the wagon train. It is only right that they be warned of the Ute's presence. I do not approve of whites settling on Wyoming land, but I do not want them slaughtered by renegades. Under the leadership of our *sachem*, Chief Half Moon, we are known for being a people of peace. Today I will speak with the whites to warn them of who might be lurking with plans of ambushing them. But first I will go and see our chief. I will bring you news of how he is faring. As each day passes, we are lucky to still have him among us."

The warriors followed Wind Walker to Chief Half Moon's lodge and dutifully waited as Wind Walker went inside.

The scent of sweet root hung heavy in the air, one of the many medicines his people used for healing. Wind Walker sat down across from his old chief, the firepit between them glowing with red embers. Chief Half Moon sat with his head somewhat bent, his eyes closed, yet he was not asleep.

Wind Walker knew that this was the way the

chief spent most of his days now. He was fighting with each and every breath to stay among those who loved and adored him. Wind Walker gazed at his chief with a love in his heart so intense it was hard to ever think of a world without him.

But Half Moon's age was very evident. His copper face was lean and lined with wrinkles. His eyes lay deep within their sockets, their dark color faded to a brownish gray.

Today his gray hair was parted in the center and worn in two thick braids wrapped in otter skin that hung long down his back. From a braided lock of his hair dangled a lone eagle feather, the insignia of a Cheyenne chief, worn instead of his headdress with its narrow beaded band, its crown covered with the gorgeous tail feathers of the golden eagle and the sides with the feathers of the hawk and crow.

Half Moon wore over his shoulder a long sash eight to ten feet long, made of deer skin that trailed behind him on the ground, called a dog rope. The dog ropes of the two bravest men of a particular clan were elaborate. Chief Half Moon's was decorated with bands of yellow and red porcupine quills and eagle feathers.

When Half Moon was twenty-five winters, he had been a Dog Soldier, one of a group of elite fighting warriors of the Cheyenne, and one of the four carriers of the *hotamtsit*, dog rope. These men were the bravest of the brave, riding at the end of the column when the camp was on the move to cover the retreat in case the clan was attacked.

The Golden Eagle Clan of Cheyenne no longer had Dog Soldiers. Since the days of Wind Walker's grandfather, peace had been their main goal, not war. But it had become hard to ensure such peace, especially with the recent attacks on whites by the Ute renegades being wrongly attributed to the Cheyenne. Though this had caused some skirmishes between the white eye cavalry and various Cheyenne hunters, no one of the Golden Eagle Clan had been forced into action, but as more forts were built on Cheyenne land, it was only a matter of time.

Wind Walker knew he had to present himself to the new arrivals. The more people who recognized that the clan was a peaceful one, the less the Cheyenne would be blamed for the atrocities performed by others.

He focused on his chief, admiring what he wore—a mountain lion robe tanned to a wondrous softness. Wind Walker knew that on the inside of the robe were depictions of Half Moon's horse-raiding and battle experiences. The chief's wife had embroidered them as he accomplished each valorous act. Half Moon had told him that he treasured the robe now that his beloved wife was gone.

Still waiting for Chief Half Moon to raise his head and open his eyes, Wind Walker gazed slowly around his chief's lodge, the largest tepee in the village. Half Moon's cache of weapons, which had not been used for many sleeps now, were laid at one side of the tepee, rolled blankets and clothes not far from them. His personal shield made from the skin of a buffalo's neck hung from a tripod just to the chief's right side. Many beautiful feathers hung from it, painted with sacred symbols that had protected him from his enemies. If one looked closely, he could see the indentions of where arrows had slammed against it. A bullet was lodged into the fabric from an enemy whom he had downed moments later with one arrow from his own powerful bow.

Half Moon slowly raised his head and peered at Wind Walker with his old eyes, as though he were having trouble seeing him.

It was a new look that Wind Walker was not accustomed to. Although his *sachem* knew him as well as he would a son, it was as though he were studying him as he might a stranger.

Wind Walker had seen this same studious gaze in the eyes of others just prior to their leaving this earth to travel to *Se-han*, the land of the dead. Surely this meant that his chief's days were numbered on this earth. Wind

Walker knew that he must grab every moment with his chief and savor it.

"*Pavevounao*, good morning, Wind Walker, my most admired warrior. You have heard my old heart beckoning to you today," Chief Half Moon said as his shoulders bent forward as though they were too heavy for him to reckon with. "It is good that you came. I have something to say. *Heaahtoveste*, listen. I have seen my death in the stars. I am not on this earth for long, and since each Cheyenne chief names his successor, it is my fervent wish that you become chief upon my death."

Chief Half Moon watched Wind Walker. As he had countless times before, he admired the young man. He was a perfect specimen of a Cheyenne warrior. He had a handsome face of nobility at his age of twenty-five winters, with set, sculpted features. He was tall and muscled with a lean, supple, sinewy body. Wind Walker had high cheekbones, a strong jaw, and a well-formed nose. His black hair was thick and coarse. He wore it long and straight down his back, tiny shells and feathers tied to a lone lock at the right side of his head.

One day soon Wind Walker would wear the headdress of *sachem*.

Today Wind Walker wore a smoke-tanned buckskin shirt that reached to his hips and moccasins of elk leather. The seam of his shirt and leggings were trimmed with tufts of horse-hair dyed in various colors. Porcupine quills were sewn to the roots of the hair.

Chief Half Moon loved Wind Walker as he would have loved his son. He had buried the child after just one winter. The only child his wife had carried within her womb. She had not been able to conceive again.

"Wind Walker, although the warriors have suspected my decision to name you chief for some time, I will nevertheless be calling them into my lodge one by one to finalize it. To make it known that you are my choice."

"I am touched deeply by your decision," Wind Walker said thickly. "*Nai-ish,* thank you, my chief. *Nai-ish.*"

Half Moon groaned as he struggled to straighten his old, tired shoulders. Then he looked into Wind Walker's eyes and smiled.

"And what does your day hold for you? The weather is good for hunting. The wind is brisk and invigorating. Too soon, snow will blanket our land as it has already the mountains. All hunts will be finished until the spring."

"*Hova-ahane,* no, I am not hunting today. I have something else on my mind," Wind Walker said. "There are more whites traveling in wagons along our land and our scouts have seen signs of Ute renegades prowling around, surely ready to cause more trouble. If the white people will allow me into their camp, I will warn them."

"Go then and see to the travelers' safety," Half Moon said. "I did the same when I was younger and the black-robed men came across our land. Although they carried what they called Bibles and spoke of Christianity to those who would listen, I saw them as no true threat. *Hee-hec*, yes, go. Be as you are, a man with a good heart. When you return, all the warriors of our village will know of my final decision that you become their *sachem*."

Wind Walker went around and knelt beside his chief and affectionately wrapped him in his powerful arms. He loved the old man so much, almost as much as he had loved his own father, who had been dead now for many moons.

"You honor me. I will make you proud when you look down from the heavens and see how I am faring as the new chief to our people," Wind Walker said thickly. He stood again and gazed down at his chief. "But you are here for many more moons to come. You are loved too much for a good-bye anytime soon."

"Your words touch this old chief's heart," Half Moon said. He reached a trembling finger to his eyes and wiped tears from them.

He gestured toward the entryway. "Go," he said. "Do as your heart bids you. My love goes with you. But first send Blue Wing in to me, for I know that you would have him ride with you today."

Wind Walker could not help but bend low and hug his old chief again. He smiled, then wheeled around and walked outside where the warriors stood waiting.

"My brethren, Chief Half Moon will soon beckon for you one by one for a private audience with him," he said. He looked to his best friend in the world, a man who had been like a brother to him since they were old enough to walk. "Blue Wing, I wish for you to ride with me. I will wait for you to have your private council with our chief. Go on inside his lodge. He awaits you. I shall ready our steeds for travel."

Blue Wing nodded as he stepped past him to enter Half Moon's lodge.

Wind Walker went to his tepee and placed his quiver of twenty arrows on his back, then slung his mighty bow with its bowstring made of twisted, strong buffalo sinew over his shoulder. He left his lodge and walked to the village corral. Wind Walker's favorite steed was a swift and clever pinto horse. He had named it Racer after the fast snake of the same name. With his speed, long mane, and sweeping tail, Racer was admired by all.

Blue Wing came up behind him with the wide stride of a proud warrior.

"My brother, the news that our *sachem* shared with me was good, even though expected," Blue Wing said. He took his horse's reins from Wind Walker. "My friend, you will be a wonderful leader, admired and loved by all. No one will challenge you for the title of chief."

"I have had the greatest of teachers in Chief Half Moon and will follow those teachings to the best of my ability," Wind Walker said, mounting his steed.

Blue Wing mounted his roan. "Under your leadership, our village will continue to prosper as it has under Chief Half Moon's guidance."

As they rode through the village Wind Walker waved at the children who ran toward him, shouting his name and waving at him. Others ran after Blue Wing, as loving toward him as toward Wind Walker. They looked to them as almost one in the same even though there soon would be a vast difference.

One would lead.

The other would follow.

They rode from the village and across vast stretches of land. Numerous streams rushed down from the freshly snow-covered mountains. The trees were bursting with autumn colors of orange, yellow, and red.

They rode past prairie dog towns. Wind Walker smiled as he saw little owls resting on some of the dirt hills of the prairie dogs while rattlesnakes coiled nearby. The dogs lived in harmony with owls in some of the holes, whereas they welcomed the rattlesnakes in others. He knew that the owls lived in these villages, as well as the snakes, because they couldn't find other shelter as good and warm.

They began riding up a slope of land that would take them to a bluff that overlooked the wagon train. They would study the wagon train first, then go and meet with the people.

The wagon train had stopped for the night, and the wagons were arranged in a wide circle, around a campfire that burned in the center. This strategy was used to protect them should there be a sudden attack from Indians. Wind Walker and Blue Wing drew a tight rein and watched the activity below them.

They didn't have long before their attention was drawn elsewhere.

Wind Walker's spine stiffened when he saw a lone white rider riding toward the wagon train. He recognized the man. He was someone that Wind Walker had learned not to trust. Wind Walker even suspected that this white man had ties with the Ute renegades, but he had no proof . . . just his gut instinct that was usually right.

"It is the white man who owns many long-horned animals," Blue Wing mumbled as his eyes also watched the man approaching the wagon train. "I wonder what his reason is for being there? Surely it is not good."

"Nothing he does is good, ever," Wind Walker said tightly. "Yet, I cannot help but have some sympathy for him. He recently lost his wife and now has two children to raise alone. Of course I pity the children more than the man, first for having such a father as he, and then to have lost a mother who was surely their only salvation in life."

Blue Wing's eyes followed the man. "Do you think he is going to warn them about renegades?"

"I cannot see that man caring about others," Wind Walker said. He laughed sarcastically. "He is a selfish, rich cattle baron who has brought his huge animals to land that once belonged solely to the red man. He has claimed too much land as his."

"*Hee-hec*, way, way too much." Blue Wing nodded.

Wind Walker tried to keep his distance from whites. After a Jesuit priest who came to live with his people was found murdered and scalped, the Golden Eagle Clan of Cheyenne had lived in dread that they would be blamed for the death. Chief Half Moon had chosen not to make a close alliance with white eyes since. His Cheyenne clan now only traded with white eyes, and even then that was done briefly at a trading post. Wind Walker himself felt safe only among people of his own kind.

But today something deep within led him to go among white eyes again. He would not feel right if he did not give them a fair warning of what might happen.

He watched and waited for the white man, Archy, to leave the wagon train. Wind Walker hoped that Archy's visit would be as brief as Wind Walker and Blue Wing's own time with them would be.

It would not take long to explain the dangers that might be lurking around the yonder bend.

Chapter 2

If certain, when this life was out—
That yours and mine should be—
I'd toss it yonder, like a Rind,
And taste Eternity—
                    —Emily Dickinson

The tantalizing aroma of meat cooking over an open fire, the juices dripping and sizzling into the flames, wafted into the air over the wagon train.

The travelers had discovered a rich store of wildlife as they traveled across the Wyoming Territory, where timber often gave way to open prairie. There had been buffalo and white-tailed deer.

Deer meat had become the preference not only because the meat was sweet and tender, but also because there were more deer and they were much easier caught and skinned than the huge buffalo.

Before leaving Boston, they had heard so much about the hairy beasts and their huge herds that grazed everywhere. But it was soon discovered that they were hardly ever seen *in* herds, that there was only just an occasional buffalo. The tales of trigger-happy white men having wiped out most of the vast herds were true, leaving hardly enough to replenish the herds. Buffalo were fast becoming a dying breed.

Margaret Ann Tolan, Maggie to those who knew her, helped spread blankets on the ground close to the fire for the evening meal.

Maggie no longer felt the excitement that she had first felt when she left Boston on the wagon train with her mother. When they had decided to make the journey to Oregon under the influence of Maggie's uncle Patrick, it had sounded like an adventure to Maggie.

Her father had died from a heart attack some years earlier, and Uncle Patrick, who was only a few years older than Maggie, had taken over the responsibilities of his late brother's wife and daughter. Leaving Boston and the sad memories that lingered over the death of her father had seemed the right thing to do. Maggie had looked forward to making a new life in a new land.

Her mother had enjoyed the journey, but Maggie had been more exuberant about it than she was. Maggie was young. At age eighteen, she had a lifetime ahead of her. She had been so happy at first. Then things began to happen that made her heart ache even now as she thought about them.

Several graves had been left along the way. The oppressive heat, snakes, spider bites, and marauding Indians who came and went quickly, had taken its toll.

Her precious mother was among those who had died.

Maggie was plagued by guilt over her mother's death. Had she not talked her mother into undertaking this trip, she would still be alive.

That particular night, her mother had been more tired than usual. She had gone to bed in their wagon before Maggie. A snake had found its way into their wagon and had curled up beneath her mother's blanket. Maggie hadn't discovered the lethal snakebite until the next morning. Her mother had died silently. She hadn't cried out! As Maggie had slid into her own blankets, her mother had already been dead.

Maggie couldn't get past her guilt. She couldn't get her mother's grave and wooden cross off her mind no matter how her uncle Patrick tried to soothe her, telling her that her mother's death was not her fault. He had tried to make Maggie understand that it had been her mother's time.

It was fate. He said one could not change or run away from fate . . . one's destiny.

Maggie didn't mingle with the women. She had no desire to discuss the journey with them as they did each evening. It only reminded her again that it was a trip she and her mother should never have taken. She preferred to stay off by herself, waiting to come to the end of their journey.

The blankets were spread, the tin plates stacked close to the fire for when the meat was ready to eat, so Maggie went off and sat down by herself. She looked for her uncle Patrick, and saw him only a few feet away, talking with several men. They got together each evening to discuss the day's affairs. Today was a good day. No fresh graves had been dug.

She settled more comfortably on the blanket and leaned her back against a wheel of her private covered wagon, as she watched her uncle. His resemblance to her father was very strong, and it hurt to look at him sometimes. It was in the jawline and shape of his head. It was the bright redness of his hair and the tiny mustache he always wore as had her father.

"Call me Red, Maggie," her uncle had insisted many years ago. "Don't call me Uncle Patrick. It makes me feel old. Call me by my nickname. Call me Red."

And so she did, although it seemed disrespectful at times, especially when they were in a group. But she complied with his wishes.

When Maggie looked into a mirror, she saw some similarities between herself and her father, as well. She had the same red hair, the same roundness to her face, the same flashing green eyes. She was glad, though, that she had not inherited the family freckles. Her face was as clear and pink as her mother's had been, and just as tiny boned. "Petite" was how many described her. Tiny, petite . . . and cute.

She hated the word *cute*.

She wanted to look dignified and elegant. She liked the word *elegant* much better than *cute*. Though it was hard to look elegant on the trail. Today, her long hair that hung down past her waist was held back from her face with wooden combs that were slid in behind her ears, and she wore a fully gathered cotton dress.

Maggie stood and walked between two wagons. Autumn was so beautiful in the Wyoming Territory. The leaves on the cottonwood and box elders were losing their waxlike summer green. Other trees were a patchwork of colors of yellow and orange. The grass on the range had dried and curled up due to the oppressive heat.

She saw a shadow on the ground and looked upward to see a lone buzzard slowly wheeling, cutting circles in the air. Maggie's eyes were quickly drawn to a magpie noisily flying past.

"Supper's on!" a lady shouted.

Another woman said jokingly, "Come and get it before we throw it to the pigs!"

The humor was welcomed by everyone. Even Maggie smiled. There were no pigs on this wagon train.

The women were congregating around the fire, some still placing bread and jars of jams and jellies on the blankets to eat with the meat. Maggie was proud to have placed her own freshly made buffalo berry jelly, known as bull-berry, among the others.

They had discovered this was the only wild fruit that grew in this part of the country. The berries were everywhere, ripe for picking, and made excellent jelly. Her mother had taught Maggie the process as a way to pass the long, lonely evenings while waiting to continue the journey the next morning.

Feeling somewhat better about things and a little hungry, Maggie went and mingled with the others, but before they sat down to eat, a sentry shouted out that a lone rider approached . . . a white man.

Everyone but Maggie hurried to see the man for themselves. She waited and watched as the man arrived on his black mustang. He was quickly invited to stay for supper and he agreed, as he came into camp.

Long, greasy, sandy-colored hair fell down across his shoulders as he lifted the wide-brimmed hat from his head and nodded a quiet hello specifically at Maggie.

He secured his horse's reins to a wheel of one of the wagons before sitting down among the people. He nodded a quiet thank-you as a lady handed him a tin plate of food.

Maggie stayed back from the others. She was leery of a lone man who just came from out of nowhere. He appeared to be in his late thirties, lean, wiry, and erect. He wore tight-waisted blue denims along with leather chaps, a pale blue hickory shirt, and a black silk bandanna around his throat. The hat he had removed and placed beside him on the ground was a Stetson of high-crowned pattern, and his black boots were scuffed and tall heeled. Around his waist he sported holstered pearl-handled pistols.

But most of all Maggie noticed his shifty eyes.

"My name's Archibald Parrish," the man said between huge bites of beans. "But my friends call me Archy."

Everyone nodded as they continued to eat. Archy looked slowly from person to person with a wicked grin on his ruddy-looking face.

"None of you have much to say," Archy said slyly. "You are my friends, ain't you?"

Maggie didn't like the wicked gleam in his pale blue eyes, nor that grin that seemed to say more than his words. Her eyes moved to his pistols. They looked as lethal as a snake's bite.

She looked up at his lean face again. It was ruddy and pockmarked. His jaw was tight and his lips were thick and held in a mocking sneer.

"Why are you traveling alone?" Red asked guardedly, placing his finished plate aside. "Isn't that dangerous out here in Indian country? Aren't you afraid of losing your scalp?"

Archy pulled a twisted rope of chewing tobacco from his shirt pocket, bit off a generous plug of it, then offered it to Red. "Have some?" he said, having slid his bite of tobacco back into one corner of his mouth, making it pooch out like a chipmunk's.

"No, don't care if I do," Red said, his voice tight with obvious wariness. He folded his arms across his chest as his eyes narrowed and he waited for the stranger's explanation.

Archy offered the tobacco to the others but none accepted. He slid it back inside his pocket, chewed awhile, then again slid the wad of tobacco back to one corner of his mouth.

"I know the land quite well and the redskins

who inhabit it," he said. "I live on homesteaded land some distance away from here.
When I saw your wagon train, I felt that I
should take the time to come and warn you
about the roaming renegades in these parts."

He slid a slow gaze over at Maggie, who still
stood away from the others. "Those renegades
are known for stealin' white women," he said
throatily. "Beautiful white women. And I've
heard that if they get their hands on one, best
kiss her good-bye. None has ever come away
alive."

Maggie felt something deep within herself
for the first time since her mother's death—
fear and mistrust. Fear of the renegades, and
mistrust for the man whose pale blue eyes
seemed to be looking clean into her soul.

There was something about him that made
her feel uneasy, but it seemed that no one else
except her uncle shared her wariness. Everyone was eager to talk and tried to hand Archy
more food and coffee. Archy seemed to forget
Maggie momentarily as he talked with the
men. Longhorns became the main topic of
Archy's conversation.

"I've got the finest longhorn ranch in these
parts," Archy bragged. "But I've not had it all
that easy keeping 'em. Those damn Injuns
sneak up and steal from right beneath my
nose."

His eyes sought Maggie again. "Yep, those Injuns steal my longhorns as cunningly and as noiselessly as they do women," he said.

He laughed and swatted at a small bug that was scarcely discernible as it landed on the sleeve of his shirt. "Those damn no-see-ums," he grumbled. "It's somethin' I'm sure you already know about, but if you don't, let me tell you, they're a helluva nuisance."

"Why is that bug called a no-see-um?" one of the ladies asked, her eyes watching Archy.

"Ma'am, I don't know any more than you do 'bout that," Archy answered. "That damn little buffalo gnat sure as hell got a name that don't match it one iota. I see and feel 'em way too often. I wish they'd stay on animals, where they belong."

As Archy's eyes shifted to Maggie again, she turned and hurried to her wagon. She stayed there until she was sure she heard Archy ride away.

Almost immediately after Archy departed, there was a loud shout from a sentry.

"Indians!" he cried. "I see Indians on the yonder bluff!"

Maggie's throat became constricted at the thought of an Indian attack. She hurried to where she could see them. A coldness surged through her. Two Indians on horseback looked down at the wagon train. She was afraid that

more would soon arrive and in a matter of moments everyone would be slaughtered!

Archy rode back to the wagon train. "Remember what I said!" he shouted. "Don't trust
any savages. Keep an eye on your women!"

Maggie was aware of his eyes searching for
her. She felt a revulsion she had never felt before. He seemed way too interested in her.

She clasped her hands tightly behind her as
she watched him ride away in the opposite direction of the Indians.

Maggie was perplexed. It seemed odd that
Archy felt safe enough to ride alone when such
dangerous Indians were near. He didn't act
worried. He had said they stole longhorns
from him, but his own safety did not come up
in the conversation. How had he survived living on Indian land?

Her jaw tight with determination, Maggie
hurried inside her wagon. She made sure that
her tiny pistol was loaded and beneath her pillow so that when she went to bed she would be
as safe as possible.

Since her mother's death, and the death of
the others on the wagon train, Maggie wondered if *any* of them would arrive in Oregon
alive.

Thunder rumbled in the distance. During
their journey, electrical storms had seemed to
come out of nowhere, but usually lasted only a

few minutes. But in a matter of minutes, things could go awry out there on this wild land. Life could be snuffed away in seconds.

Maggie had lost five of her friends when a storm spooked some of the horses on the wagon train. Their team had galloped away in a frenzy, the wagon still attached. As the wagon came loose, it toppled over and shattered into a million pieces down a steep ravine.

Uncle Red rode in the wagon ahead of her, leaving Maggie to handle her own team. Maggie could not help but be afraid when she heard storms approaching as the wagon traveled across straight stretches of land, making them vulnerable to lightning strikes.

Now when she heard thunder and saw lurid flashes of lightning, she got almost sick to her stomach. Combined with the possibility of an Indian attack, her fear of dying almost overwhelmed her.

Her throat went dry when she heard the sentries shout that the two Indians were now approaching. Maggie could feel the color drain from her face and her pulse begin to race. Could this be a part of those renegades Archy had warned them about?

She gazed heavenward. "Please, oh, please protect us from harm," she prayed.

Chapter 3

Shall I compare thee to a summer's day?
Thou art more lovely and more temperate.
                                    —William Shakespeare

As Wind Walker rode toward the circle of wagons, he watched Archy ride in the opposite direction. He did not trust that man.

He turned to look at the white men who had stepped outside of the circle of wagons. Weapons in hand, they watched the approach of what most people called their enemy.

Wind Walker knew that one of those travelers could shoot him and Blue Wing out of fear, but as long as they did nothing threatening toward the white people, Wind Walker was sure they would not do anything rash. Killing two red men would only cause many more to come to avenge their brethren's deaths.

Believing that nothing would happen to him, Wind Walker rode onward. When he came within shouting range, he drew Racer to a halt. Blue Wing stopped his roan beside him.

"My name is Wind Walker and my friend is Blue Wing. Do not be alarmed by our presence," Wind Walker shouted in fluent English. "We come in peace and friendship. Trust me when I say that there are only the two of us. Will you accept us among you to talk?"

Maggie stepped between her wagon and the one next to it far enough to be able to see the Indians. They seemed friendly enough, and there *were* only the two of them. She looked to the bluff for signs of any more. There were none. She felt assured that this warrior spoke the truth.

And there was something else about him. Maggie couldn't keep her eyes off of him as her uncle invited them into the camp. She had never encountered such a handsome man. Of all the red-skinned men she had seen on the journey thus far, she had seen only scruffy renegades. But Maggie could tell that this man was noble. It was the way he held himself so straight, so erect, in the saddle. His fine voice spoke the English language fluently and exact. Surely he was among those few Indians who did not seek warring with whites.

She watched as he and the other Indian dismounted, then stepped through a space between two wagons several feet away from where she stood.

Lured by the mystique of Wind Walker, by his unique handsomeness, Maggie hurried to sit beside her uncle. The Indians sat down on the opposite side of the campfire, close enough for her to see the intensity of Wind Walker's midnight-dark eyes, the loveliness of his copper skin, and the sculpted features of his face.

Maggie's eyes roamed over his powerful, muscled build, his long black hair, his beautiful beaded buckskin attire.

"Would you like a plate of food, or a cup of coffee?" Red asked as he looked from Wind Walker to Blue Wing then back to Wind Walker.

"Yes, food and drink is good," Wind Walker said, making sure he continued to speak in English.

He nodded a thank-you to a woman as she handed him food on a tin plate and a tin cup of coffee, which in truth, he loathed.

But to prove that he was there in friendship, and not to insult his host, he took a sip of the bitter black liquid called coffee.

Blue Wing ate while surveying the travelers. He was aware of the uneasiness all around him, especially among the women. Some of them were wringing their hands or strangely chewing on their lower lip. Their children were clinging to them, some sobbing in fear.

He gazed over at Wind Walker to see how he was reacting to their behavior and saw no sign of it affecting him, proving to Blue Wing again that he was a leader to be admired and loved by all.

Maggie peeked at her uncle. He sat stiffly, his gaze never leaving Wind Walker. She could tell that he was uneasy at the Indians' presence, yet was trying hard not to show it. He was the leader of this wagon train. Everything and everyone's safety seemed to rest on his broad shoulders.

If he made a wrong decision . . .

She looked over at the Indians again. They had emptied their plates, as well as their cups, and had set them aside. They folded their arms across their chests, yet not in a tight, threatening way.

"We have come today in friendship to warn you about renegades," Wind Walker said, his eyes flicking to the flame-haired woman who sat at the man's right side.

He tried hard not to stare. It would be dangerous if the white eyes saw him taking a slightest bit of interest in one of their women. He forced himself to keep his eyes on the man whose name was Red.

"Keep a close watch at all times," he said.

"The renegades have murdered white travelers."

Maggie enjoyed listening to the warrior's voice and gazing at his handsomeness. She was intrigued . . . mesmerized. But she had to remind herself that this man was not any ordinary man. He was an Indian.

She had heard horror stories about Indian warriors and the atrocities they performed against white women after they abducted them. A cold shiver rode her spine just thinking about it.

But surely this gentle-speaking man was not capable of such monstrosities. His eyes showed no resentment of whites; his actions revealed no threat. He seemed kind.

Maggie warned herself to stop thinking about him. Soon he would be gone and she would be on her way to Oregon. They would never cross paths again.

Wind Walker's battle within was lost. He could not help but finally slide his eyes over to the white woman. Their eyes locked and momentarily held, and Wind Walker felt something stir deep inside him.

Her loveliness caused feelings in him that he knew were wrong. Only one other time had he seen such a beautiful woman—Sweet Willow, his wife.

He wanted to ask her name, but knew the whites fiercely protected their women from red-skinned men. It was forbidden to talk to them.

He quickly looked away from her, glad that Blue Wing was conversing with the flame-haired man, diverting attention from Wind Walker. Surely no one had noticed his attention, his attraction, to the woman.

But now, even when he was not looking at her, he could not stop the feelings that were awakened by her mere presence. Feelings that he thought had died with Sweet Willow three moons ago. They had not slept a full night as man and wife before the hand of fate struck them a deadly blow. As Sweet Willow had sat beside a stream washing her hair before joining him on their wedding night, a storm that had lingered in the distant hills for some time had come suddenly like a raging beast. Thunder roared and shook the earth. A bolt of lightning had struck and fell the tree she had knelt beside, killing her instantly.

Wind Walker left offerings at the site of the dead tree. He believed its spirit joined hers after the deadly attack from the heavens.

Hee-hec, there was something about this flame-haired woman that reminded him of his Sweet Willow.

Suddenly he rose to his feet. He could no

longer stay where dangerous feelings had been aroused.

"We must go," Wind Walker said thickly. "Our duty here is done. We must return to our own people. But I hope you have listened to my warning. Renegades can come like ghosts in the night, wreaking havoc along the way. Watch. Listen. Protect those you love with all that you have."

Red stood up and walked with Wind Walker and Blue Wing to their steeds. Before Wind Walker mounted Racer, he extended a hand of friendship toward Red.

"It was good to have dialogue with a man of your countenance," he said. "Travel with care. May *Maheo* . . . may *your* God . . . keep you safe until you arrive at your destination."

"Thank you," Red said, accepting the handshake. "I do appreciate your warning and your kindness."

Wind Walker smiled, eased his hand away, then swung himself into his saddle. Aware that the red-haired woman stood between wagons, watching him, Wind Walker fought against looking back at her. Instead, he wheeled his horse around and rode off with Blue Wing at a hard gallop.

Maggie continued to watch Wind Walker as he rode away, remembering how their eyes had met and held. He had looked at her long enough for her to know that he found her intriguing. It was in his midnight-dark eyes.

It gave her a sensual thrill to consider what that look meant.

"Maggie?" Her uncle's voice brought her out of her trance.

She turned and found Red standing behind her with a strange look in his eyes, as though he had read her thoughts and knew she was thinking about something . . . someone . . . very forbidden.

She felt the rush of color in her cheeks as she looked sheepishly back at him.

"Things'll be all right," he said, drawing her into his gentle embrace. "Maggie, my sweet Magpie, I can tell by the way you are behaving that you were frightened by the Indians. You shouldn't be. They seemed genuinely friendly, even kind."

Maggie was relieved that he had misread her behavior. She returned the hug.

"I trust that you will keep me safe enough," she said. "I love you, Uncle Patrick. I love you so much."

"Hey now, what is this?" he said, holding her away from him and smiling into her eyes. "I'm suddenly that old man—an uncle—again? Where did the name Red go?"

"I'm sorry," Maggie giggled. "Red. Yes, Red. I don't know why I called you Uncle Patrick."

"Well, I do," Red said, nodding. "It's because you *were* feeling threatened by those Indians and you felt safer with an 'older' man. Am I right? When you call me Uncle Patrick you see me as older and more dependable?"

"Certainly not," Maggie said, laughing softly. She took his hand. "Come on. Let's rejoin the others."

"Sweet Magpie," he said, using the nickname he had given her long ago. He stopped and turned her to face him. "Will you rest tonight? Are you feeling safe?"

"As safe as one can feel with renegades out there," Maggie said.

"Well, you know what you must do, don't you?" Red asked seriously.

"Yes. Keep my pistol handy and shoot to kill if I have to," she answered.

"That's my girl," Red said, smiling into her eyes. "I've taught you well."

"I hope so," Maggie said as she took his hand and they went to join the others around the campfire.

Red warned everyone to prepare themselves for a long night, to be sure to keep a closer watch than usual. Maggie couldn't shake the sense of foreboding that came with the warning. She knew that her uncle was referring to the redskin renegades.

Maggie looked at the women who were still cleaning up. There was a strained look in their eyes and a quietness about them. She felt the same sort of feeling in her heart when she thought of Wind Walker's warnings about renegades.

Maggie went to her wagon and changed into her warm, long flannel nightgown.

Her mind drifted to Wind Walker and for a moment she felt a strange deliciousness warming her. The man had had an effect on her and she knew that it would be some time before she could get over it.

Yawning, she slipped beneath her quilts. As she ran her hand over the patchwork quilt, tears welled up in her eyes. Her mother had made the quilt from scraps of her discarded dresses. It seemed impossible to believe that she would never feel her mother's loving arms around her again, or hear her soft voice.

"I'm sorry, Mama," she whispered.

Maggie wished she had been more attentive that night. She should have at least checked on her mother before she had bedded down. If she could have found her mother moments after she was bitten, perhaps she could have saved her.

But that night, Maggie had been weary from

the long, hot day of travel. Her mother had gone to bed before her, and Maggie had not thought to check on her.

Thunder rumbled far up in the mountains. She had never felt as alone or as dispirited.

Chapter 4

Many waters cannot quench love,
Neither can the floods drown it.
                              —King Solomon

Maggie could not fall asleep no matter how hard she tried. She kept going over everything in her mind. But at least her tears had stopped. She was reconciling herself to the fact that there was nothing she could have done to prevent her mother's death.

Sighing, she threw back the quilt. Pulling the hem of her nightgown up past her knees, she crawled to the back of the wagon and stopped and gazed from it.

There was no longer any rumbling thunder in the mountains. Everything was peacefully quiet. The air was sweet and invigorating from the passing storm.

If she closed her eyes, she could imagine that she was back in Boston, stepping out onto the front porch around midnight to sit in the porch swing alone, the way it had been before her father and now, her mother, had died. She wondered if life could ever be that simple again.

Gazing up at the dark sky, Maggie sought one of the twinkling stars that flashed like a tiny lantern. She smiled and repeated something that she had said so often as a little girl in Boston.

"I wish I may, I wish I might, have my first wish I wish tonight." She lowered her eyes, then whispered, "I truly wish that I could be happy again."

Feeling the heat of tears building in her eyes again, Maggie crawled back to her blankets and drew the quilt up over her. Finally she relaxed and fell into the black void of sleep where she found the solace and escape she so badly hoped for tonight.

Maggie was awakened abruptly as a hand clasped over her mouth and she felt the sharp, cold steel of a knifepoint at the nape of her neck. A coldness settled around her heart when a voice spoke to her. It was so low she could not recognize it. But she knew that it was a man.

"Come with me and do not cry out," the voice whispered into her ear as he yanked her up from her blankets and forced her to stand in front of him, his arm holding her hostage against him. "You'd best do what I tell you. My knife can silence you very quickly."

Knowing that she had no choice, she left the wagon and was told to go straight ahead between two others. The moon was covered by the passing storm clouds, so it was too dark to see her abductor. The man who had posted guard was unconscious on the ground. She couldn't see who it was, and prayed that it was not her uncle. She prayed to herself that he was not dead.

She was forced onward. The knife continuously held at the nape of her neck was a crude reminder that she could not break free.

As they reached a stand of cottonwood trees, her abductor warned her to be quiet and not to try to run. Maggie's knees trembled as he tied a gag around her mouth, then tied her hands behind her.

She was spun around just as the moon broke free of the clouds. Her heart sank when she saw who her assailant was.

Archy!

He grabbed her by the waist and lifted her onto his horse, then mounted behind her, one of his arms locking her in place against him.

They rode for a while, then Archy drew a tight rein and stopped his black stallion. He removed his arm and gave her a shove. "Git," he growled. "Get down from my horse. Don't try to run away. You can't get far."

Maggie did as she was told. Her knees were trembling so violently she found it hard to stand. Her heart was pounding away, as though sledgehammers were inside her.

When he reached out and yanked the gag from her mouth, she licked her parched lips, ready to scream as loud as she possibly could. He laughed into her face.

"You can scream now, if you have a mind to," he said. "But it's useless. We are too far from the wagon train for anyone to hear you, and there ain't nothing else around here 'cept the Cheyenne village, and that is still too far away."

He leaned into her face, sneering. "Maybe you *should* scream. There just might be a renegade or two out there who'd like to take a turn or two with you."

The color quickly drained from Maggie's face, and she fought back the urge to vomit. She tightened her jaw, lifted her chin defiantly, and stared angrily into the man's evil eyes.

"Why have you taken me from the wagon train?" she asked, her voice dry and tight. "Are you going to rape me?"

"Naw, I have no intention of raping you," he said, laughing throatily. "But in time you *will* go to bed with me."

She spat at his feet.

"Well, now, look at you," Archy laughed boisterously. "I like a woman with spirit. Yes, ma'am, you are going to work out just fine for me."

"Why have you abducted me?" she asked, her voice breaking. "Why would you do such a thing? You could hang for it."

"I don't reckon I have that to worry about," Archy said, placing his fists on his hips. "I'll not allow you to escape to tell what's happened. And I took you because I'm a wealthy rancher with many longhorn cattle and many cowhands who work for me. I need a woman to cook for them."

"That's why you abducted me?" she asked, her eyes widening. "Why didn't you find a woman the legal way?"

"Out here women are scarce," he said. "Not many men have the guts to have a ranch near Indians like I do, and most wouldn't bring a wife with him to a godless country."

He momentarily lowered his eyes. "I had me a wife," he said somberly. "She died recently. I've been left to look after our two kids. I have a four-year-old son named Jeremy and a ten-year-old named Kevin. I need a woman for them, as well as my cowhands. I came to the wagon train to look the women over. I chose you, but knew you wouldn't come willingly. I had no choice but to take what I wanted, not waste time in askin'."

"You've got to know that I'll never stay," Maggie said. She challenged him with a set, angry, stubborn stare. "I'll find a way to escape at my first opportunity."

"That's no concern of mine," he said, idly shrugging. "You'll be watched twenty-four hours a day. Even if you do somehow manage to elude those who are keepin' an eye on you, you won't get far."

"You're a fiend," Maggie said.

"No, just a daddy lookin' after the needs of his kids and those who work for him." He leaned his face close to hers. "You can cook, cain't you?"

She refused to reply.

"Be stubborn," he said, shrugging again. "I know you can cook. All women cook!"

Maggie tightened as he swept her into his arms and placed her on the horse again, then rode onward through the dark-shadowed night.

"My uncle Red won't rest until he finds me," Maggie challenged.

"That man's your uncle, huh? Well, just let him try to find you," Archy answered. "I'd be the last person he'd think about. He'll blame everything on Injuns. I planted the seed about how they enjoy stealin' pretty white women. I could tell he took the bait. And I left a calling card in your wagon."

"What sort of calling card?" Maggie asked guardedly.

"An arrow," Archy said matter-of-factly. "A broken arrow, the sort the Cheyenne use. I'm sick to death of those Cheyenne."

"Where did you get a Cheyenne arrow?" Maggie asked, her voice hard. She hated that the wrong man would be accused of tonight's crime—a man who seemed too gentle to even consider abducting an innocent woman.

"I found it along the trail. Broken or not I knew one day it would serve a purpose. An arrow is an arrow."

Maggie's heart sank to know that he had planned tonight's abduction very well. Unless her uncle saw the same cruelty in Archy's eyes that she had seen, he would seek the wrong man. Her uncle was her only hope. Otherwise, she had no idea what was going to happen to her.

She said nothing more as Archy rode onward, her head jerking up when he told her that they were arriving at his ranch.

The moon had broken free of the clouds, allowing Maggie to see how immense the ranch was. His rambling house sat amidst a rolling, wooded acreage. And the longhorns! She had never seen any before now. She was in awe of the beasts and the amount he owned.

Archy saw how taken Maggie was. It was in her eyes and her low gasp.

"I've homesteaded this piece of land for some time now," he said proudly. "I call it my heaven on earth. Cattle ranching is a good business. The only disadvantage is that the longhorn breed have an extraordinary wildness about them that makes them nervous and easy to stampede. Their thick horns are set forward and can be as sharp as knives."

As he rode toward the house, he pointed one out to her. "See that one? That's a great brindle bull. It's seven years old and at the apex of its prowess."

Maggie stared at the bull. It was mighty-antlered and wild-eyed. Its powerful neck showed a great bulge just behind the head, a big dewlap accenting its primeval origin. And its horns were most threatening in size!

It seemed to be challenging Archy with a set stare, its eyes gleaming and burning like a bull's-eye lantern. It was pawing dirt, lifting it with its forefeet so that it went high up in the air and fell in part upon its own back.

It stopped to hook its master horn into the ground, goring down to a clayish damp that stuck to the tip. Then it hooked both horns in, one at a time, and, kneeling, rubbed its shoulder against the ground. Its powerful lungs huffed out streams of breath that sprayed particles of earth away from its nostrils.

Standing with earth plastering its horns, matting its shaggy frontlet, and covering its back from head to toe, the longhorn's head swayed. Hoarse and deep, like thunder on the horizon, it rumbled *uh huh uh uh whing* before raising its head in a loud, high defiant challenge, combining a bellow with a shriek.

Maggie sighed with relief as the longhorn wheeled around and ran off in the opposite direction.

Archy chuckled. "There's bad blood between me and that particular bull," he said, watching as the longhorn stopped and stood with others of his own size and stature.

"Really?" Maggie said, smiling wickedly over her shoulder at Archy. "Seems that bull is a good judge of character."

"Well, I'm not so sure 'bout that," Archy said, as he rode up to the house and drew a tight rein.

Maggie looked again at the massive house, then over her shoulder at what she assumed was the cowhands' bunkhouse. She hated to think of just how many men were under this madman's employ. What if they were as evil as Archy? She shuddered at the possibility.

"This will be the first place my uncle will

look for me," she said. She turned and glared at him. She placed her hands on her hips.

"As I recall, you didn't hide your interest in me when you came and introduced yourself to everyone at the wagon train," she said, smirking. "I didn't see you look at any other woman. My uncle is an astute man. I'm sure he saw your keen interest in me.

"I'm certain he was aware of how quickly I got up and went to my wagon and surmised why," she said cunningly. "Your little game of leaving an arrow in my bed won't work. It'll be looked at as just what it is—a plant."

"Shows what you know about men," Archy said, dismounting. "All men who see you would show interest. Surely your uncle has seen it everywhere you go. He wouldn't think anything about how I looked at you."

He leaned into her face. "And the planted arrow *will* do the trick," he snarled. "Your uncle will blame Injuns and everyone knows better than to go up against savages. He will just have to accept his loss and move on without you."

"He'd never do that," Maggie said, her eyes gleaming into his. "He *will* come looking for me. When he finds me, you'll regret having ever taken me."

"Let him come," Archy said, flinging his reins around a hitching rail. "I have men posted. They keep watch for any strangers that are seen approaching my ranch."

A sudden fear swept through her heart. If her uncle did come, he might not be allowed to leave alive.

Archy grabbed her hard by a wrist and half dragged her up the steep front steps, then gave her a push into his house when he got the door open. He shoved her down a long corridor, then into a room and left, locking the door behind her.

She didn't have time to look around before Archy was back with a basin of water and a clean nightgown, and a dress that he said had been his wife's.

"Clean yourself up, sleep, and then you'll meet my kids tomorrow," he said. He leaned forward and smiled even more wickedly. "And then you'll prepare all of my men, myself, and my children a breakfast that'll be fit for a king."

He gazed more intensely into her eyes. "A name," he said tightly. "I need a name to go with that pretty face and red hair."

Maggie stubbornly didn't tell him.

He reached around and grabbed her by her hair. He leaned into her face. "A name," he growled. "Or do I have to beat it outta you?"

A coldness rushed up and down Maggie's spine as she looked into his demonic eyes.

"Margaret Ann Tolan," she gulped. "But my friends call me Maggie."

"Then count me in as a friend, *Maggie*," he said, his eyes gleaming. "'Cause that's how I'll be introducin' you to my kids *and* the gents who work at my ranch."

He laughed cynically as he released his hold on her hair and walked away from her. He closed the door and locked it, leaving Maggie alone, her throat constricting as she fought back a strong urge to cry. She couldn't believe this was happening to her.

And then she thought of this man's children—how horrible it would be to have a father like Archy!

The moon hung over the ragged-edged mountains in the distance. Wind Walker walked beside the river and stopped at the bent, charred willow tree where his wife had died.

A loon sung from the purple thistle, its song echoing eerily over the quiet waters of the river. Wolves howled on a close-by ridge. The river whispered as it flowed past, the reflected moon making a path of white.

He had all of these sounds inside his heart, but he heard only the great clap of thunder after the lightning had struck the tree that fateful night. Its fire reached over and claimed his beautiful wife's life at the same time as the tree's.

Kneeling, he prayed as he placed offerings on what remained of the small willow tree's limbs. He had brought beads tonight, as well as a small strip of fur that he had taken from a rabbit.

He always felt his wife's presence when he knelt beside the tree. But tonight he felt drawn from those thoughts as another woman's face came to his mind's eye—a woman whose face was white.

Feeling as though he were betraying his wife's memory, he blinked his eyes and fought off the images.

Yet, as he rose to walk back to his lodge, again her face rose up, strangely haunting him. He felt that something might be wrong.

Was she, the woman from the wagon train whose eyes had momentarily captured his heart, in danger?

Chapter 5

If thou love'st me too much,
'Twill not prove as true a touch;
Love me little more than such—
For I fear the end.
                    —Anonymous

Panic seized Red as he looked into Maggie's wagon after she hadn't come out for breakfast. He turned abruptly and ran to where everyone was congregating around the morning campfire, coffee already sending its delicious aroma into the air.

He looked quickly all around him. He hoped that she had gone around one side of her wagon as he had come from the other. If so, she should be with the women, helping organize the breakfast plates and pouring coffee. But his heart went cold when he still didn't see her anywhere.

His face flushed with fear, he shouted out Maggie's name, hoping that she was somewhere close by. Everyone stopped and turned to gaze at him, a fearful question in their eyes.

"Has anyone seen Maggie this morning?" Red asked, his voice lower, his throat dry. "I just checked her wagon. She isn't there."

When no one spoke up, Red realized his worst fear may have come to pass. Someone had come under the cover of darkness and abducted her.

Without saying anything else, he broke into a run and went to where a sentry had been posted close to Maggie's wagon.

His heart sank and his knees grew weak when he found the sentry beneath her wagon, where someone had shoved him after rendering him unconscious. He fell to his knees and crawled beneath the wagon to check on the man.

Red was relieved when he discovered that the sentry was alive, but he wasn't sure for how much longer. The man had a severe wound to his head where someone had hit him. Blood had pooled beneath his golden hair.

"Come and help me!" he cried, not realizing that everyone had followed him and stood watching with eyes filled with fear. He looked over his shoulder as two men came crawling toward him.

Soon Adam Trent was beside the morning fire on thick blankets, his head wound cleansed and medicated, a clean shirt replacing the one that had been bloodied. There wasn't a doctor in the wagon train, but several men and women knew what to do in case of an emergency.

Clarence Klein knelt beside Adam, winding a bandage around his head. He smiled as Adam's eyelashes fluttered. "He's waking!" he announced. "Adam, can you hear me?"

Adam winced, then cried out when he became fully conscious. He reached up and found the bandage around his head. "What happened?" he asked.

"You can't remember?" Clarence asked, looking quickly over at Red as he knelt beside him.

"Adam, my niece is gone," Red said. "Surely whoever took her did this to you. Can't you remember anything?"

Adam sighed heavily. "No, I'm sorry, I can't. I don't even remember being hit."

Red became lost in thought. He remembered the Indian named Wind Walker and the man named Archy staring openly at Maggie yesterday. But he couldn't imagine the white man doing anything as foolish as abducting a woman.

Then there was Wind Walker. Had he come to introduce himself as a ploy, while choosing which woman to steal from the wagon train?

"Red!"

Mick Womack came running from Maggie's wagon. He was waving two pieces of an arrow in the air. "I found this in her wagon! An Indian arrow. It must have fell from an Indian's quiver and broke as he wrestled Maggie. Whoever did this was an Indian. But which ones? Ute renegades—or Cheyenne?"

Red took the arrow pieces from Mick as he stopped before him. "Good Lord," he said, paling. "We were warned about renegades by both the Cheyenne warrior and Archy."

"Then you think a savage did this . . . a renegade?" one of the women asked, her voice thin with fear.

"One can't be sure," Red said, still studying the arrow pieces.

He thought back to both men who came yesterday and showed interest in Maggie. The arrow proved it couldn't have been Archy. But even though it was an Indian arrow, he just could not believe that such a gentle-acting man as Wind Walker could do such a fiendish thing. If he had, he was a damn good actor to have tricked Red.

"What are we to do?" Mick Womack asked, his voice trembling.

"Well, I know one thing. There aren't enough men here to stand up against the redskins," Red answered. "I'm not sure how far we'd have to travel to get to Fort Bent, the next place shown on my map where we might get some help."

He sighed heavily. "That leaves only one thing that we *can* do. We've got to find her ourselves, but we need help. I say we look for Archy's ranch."

Though Red felt that Archy was not a likable man and seemed to be putting on an act of kindness, he had no choice but to ask for his help. And if Archy's ranch was as large as he had bragged, he had to have a few cattlemen who would willingly give a helping hand when they heard of an innocent woman's abduction.

Again he thought about the Ute renegades. They *could* be the ones who had cunningly come in the night and stolen Maggie away. Red and his friends would be taking a chance out on strange land with renegades who might be waiting to kill them.

Red tightened his jaw. He had to throw caution to the wind. He *must* find Maggie at all cost!

He looked from man to man. "Who is willing to ride with me to find Maggie?" he shouted, his fists on his hips. "We'll leave as many men as we can here at the wagon train to protect the women. But I *am* going to search for my niece!"

He felt a surge of pride swell in his chest as each man stepped forward.

He went and clasped hands with them, then chose the ones who should stay behind.

"It's up to you to keep the women safe," he said.

The men nodded and reassured him that they would make certain the women would be kept from harm if Ute renegades arrived.

Soon those who were leaving had their horses saddled and their weapons ready. Red placed the broken arrow in his saddlebag, then mounted his own mare. He looked from man to man, and woman to woman, then gazed down at Adam who was still lying on blankets beside the fire. He wheeled his horse around and rode from the circle of wagons, his friends following on their own powerful steeds.

The wagons were quickly far behind them. Red and the men rode past red cactus in bloom where prickly pear grew in profusion and nettle with lovely white blossoms and petals like tissue paper. In the distance, the foothills lay in deep purple shadow. All this beauty contrasted against how Red felt.

His niece. Where was she? Was she still alive?

A surge of guilt swept through Red to think that he might have lost Maggie. He had already lost his brother's wife on this journey that he had planned and encouraged so many to join.

He would never forget the excitement in Maggie's eyes when he had first told her about taking a wagon train from Boston to a land of promise and beauty called Oregon. Nor could he forget the fear in Maggie's mother's eyes when she had finally agreed to join them. Now his eagerness to begin a new life elsewhere could have cost him his wonderful niece's life.

"Oh, please let her be alive," he whispered, gazing heavenward at a sky so blue and so serene, it seemed as though one should be able to reach up and caress it.

He wondered if Maggie might be gazing up at that same sky. What could she be doing? Who was she with?

He would not give up believing that she was still alive!

Chapter 6

I with thee have fixed my lot,
Certain to undergo like doom; if death
Consort with thee, death is to me as life.
                                        —John Milton

Maggie awakened to the bawling of cattle. She already realized that when the longhorns were not eating or sleeping, they were bellowing, moaning, and making all sorts of ungodly noises.

Hearing the longhorns made her realize once again where she was and that she was the prisoner of a madman. She wasn't certain what to expect today. She was just grateful that he had left her alone for the rest of the night and that she had been able to finally fall asleep and forget for a while that everything in her life had changed since she left Boston.

"Ma'am?"

A tiny voice beside the bed brought Maggie's eyes quickly around. Two children were standing there. She sat up and gazed at them. She recalled Archy telling her that he had two sons. Jeremy was four, and Kevin was ten.

She noticed how shabbily they were dressed. Their hair was long and dirty, their eyes revealing a haunted loneliness.

"Why, hello," Maggie murmured, smiling at them as she pulled the blanket up and around her. "My name's Maggie. What's yours?"

"I'm hungry," the younger of the two blurted out instead of answering her question. "Pa told me you'd be cooking breakfast. Will you cook it now?"

The other one seemed more interested in something besides food. He had his own question to ask. His wary dark eyes intensely gazed back at her.

"Where did you come from?" Kevin asked. "How do you know my Pa?"

Maggie was surprised by his abruptness and was torn about what to say. The children probably weren't aware of their father's dark side, so how could they understand his abducting her? They had surely been traumatized enough by the death of their mother without having to know the awful truth about their father.

She searched for signs of mistreatment, but thankfully didn't see any bruises. However, the state of their clothing and the emptiness in their eyes proved that their life was anything but happy.

She had no choice but to ignore Kevin's question, for he would be alarmed by the answer. "If you children will leave the room for a moment, I'll get dressed," Maggie said. "Then I'll be happy to get you some breakfast."

Her own stomach suddenly growled and the noise brought a soft smile to the boys' lips.

"Ma'am," Jeremy said, his smile gone, his eyes studying her. "Are you going to be our mommy? I've missed having a mommy. Since ours died, the only person who cooks and cleans and takes care of us is Cookie. He was a cowhand."

Maggie was reminded of her own mother and how much she missed her. She felt their loss and was drawn to them, but knew it was dangerous. She wouldn't be staying. She would either find a way to escape, or her uncle would find her.

"No, I'm not going to be your mommy," she answered softly. "I won't be here for long."

"Where are you going?" Jeremy asked. "Why did you come only to leave again?"

Archy came into the room in time to save her from a question she didn't know how to answer. If they knew the real answer, they would see their father as a monster.

She wished she could tell them to ask their

"Pa," but refrained from doing anything that would further confuse the children.

"That's enough," Archy grumbled. He gestured with a hand toward the door. "Scat, you brats. Get outta here. Don't you know when a lady needs her privacy?"

"But I'm hungry, Pa," Jeremy whined.

"Well, if you don't leave, Maggie won't be able to get breakfast ready for you. She's the cook now, not Cookie," Archy said, trying to look affectionate as he playfully tousled his younger son's golden hair. "Run along. When you smell bacon and eggs a'cookin', then you'll know it's time to eat."

The two children gave Maggie a strange look, then ran hand in hand from the room.

"What'd you tell them before I came into the room?" Archy demanded as he placed his fists on his hips. "You know better'n to tell them the truth, don't cha?"

"I didn't tell them anything except my name," Maggie said dryly. "I didn't think it wise to tell them that you're a fiend. But I'm sure they'll learn soon enough. I'd hate to think what will become of them then."

"Just you shut up," Archy growled. "I don't want to hear any more of your chitchat. You've been brought here to do a job. Git up and do it. My cowhands are tired of the grub Cookie has prepared. They're hungry for a woman's touch in the kitchen."

"I won't leave this bed while you're in the room," Maggie said, glaring up at him as she clutched the blanket more closely to her.

"Well, all right." Archy nodded. "I'll be just outside the door, so don't try anything funny, do you hear? There ain't no way in hell you're going to escape me."

Maggie defied him with a set, cold stare that he seemed to cower beneath before he backed his way out of the room and closed the door to give her privacy.

Soon she was dressed in a soft cotton dress and in the kitchen. The minute she had put the dress on, she smelled something she couldn't identify. Even as she cooked the great slabs of bacon, she could smell it. Maggie could only surmise that it was the smell of his wife.

She shivered at the thought of wearing a dead woman's clothes, perhaps unwashed since she had last worn it. But it was better than wearing what she had been taken in—a nightgown.

She kept reminding herself that she wouldn't be wearing it for long. She just knew that her uncle would rescue her. Hopefully before nightfall.

"Come on," Archy grumbled as he stamped

into the kitchen. "Make it snappy. The men are waiting."

"You've not said yet how many men I'm to cook for." Maggie pushed a fallen lock of her hair back from her sweaty brow. The cookstove was hot as she stood over it.

"Thirty," Archy said matter-of-factly, grabbing a piece of cooked bacon from a platter and shoving the whole thing into his mouth, then chewing it noisily.

Maggie almost dropped the wooden spatula when she heard the enormity of the job assigned to her. Her eyes widened at the thought of having to cook for so many men.

She wasn't certain she could do it. She was used to cooking for only two or three people.

"Quit pokin' around," Archy spat out at her. "Time's a wastin'. And be sure to make lots of coffee and biscuits. You've got hungry men to feed, and once you get this meal finished, you've got the noon meal to figure out. I want food that sticks to the ribs, do you hear?"

He chuckled when he pointed out the circles beneath her eyes. "Got no sleep last night, huh?" he taunted.

"How could I?" Maggie shot back at him, while turning the bacon, then making room for more in the huge iron skillet. "I had to listen to the longhorns all night. Don't they sleep?"

"Yep, but certain things wake 'em up. It's

called 'cow talk,'" he said, nodding. "A cow has one moo for her newborn calf, another for when it's older, one to tell it to come to her side, and another to tell it to stay hidden in tall grass."

He leaned his ear toward the window. "The bawling and lowing of my longhorns are music to my ears," he said.

He grabbed her arm, causing her to drop the spatula into the skillet, and jerked her to the window. "Just look at 'em," he said proudly. "Look at those glistening, curved horns. They're a sight for these old, proud eyes, and what a profitable business they are. Their meat sells for three cents a pound. Watch now. Look at those men on horseback. Some of them are already at work. The cows and calves are being cut from the main herd for branding."

He released her arm, but blocked her way so that she couldn't return to the stove even though she knew that he could smell the scorched bacon the same as she could.

"The best cutting ponies are so alert and intelligent their riders have little need of reins," Archy then said. "As soon as the cowhand shows the pony which calf or steer he wants to cut, the horse's ears begin to twitch and its eyes stay glued to the animal as it's chased to the branding iron. It knows what it's doing."

He chuckled. "See how that one cowhand is

heating the branding iron to a red-hot glow?
Watch those two men on horseback roping that
calf by the hind legs. See how they're now
dragging it toward the fire? They're working in
teams. One wrestles the calf to the ground
while the other brands it on the ribs, and another man steps up and dehorns the animal."

"Now watch the other man as he castrates
the critter," he said, laughing boisterously
when he heard Maggie gasp at the sight, then
saw her look away.

"All right, enough of this," he said and
yanked her back to the stove. "Let's get this
show on the road. Let's get the rest of the food
cookin'."

Maggie was glad when he left the room. She
sweated and cursed beneath her breath as she
finished cooking huge plates of bacon, eggs,
and biscuits, and filled large pots with freshly
brewed coffee.

Soon she was serving the rough-looking
cowhands, whose eyes showed their apprecia-
tion. One told her that she was mighty good to
look at and that he liked seeing her more than
the food she was serving them.

She was getting more uneasy by the minute,
and was relieved when they were finally finished eating so she could see to the ungodly
mess.

Needing a breath of fresh air before she

started gathering the dishes from the table for washing, she stepped from the back door. She was again awed by the longhorns and the lush grounds that belonged to Archy.

Several longhorns were grazing on a pasture of purple alfalfa. Most of the longhorns' coarse-haired coat was a glossy, dunnish brown merging into black, with white speckles and splotches on their rumps and a washed-out copper line down their backs. They were tall, bony, flat-sided, thin-flanked, and grotesquely narrow-hipped. Their length was extended, their backs swayed, their big ears curved into outlandish design. There seemed to be a gleam in most of the large animals' eyes.

She turned her attention to the many men who were doing their duties. None of them seemed trustworthy enough for her to be comfortable around them. That meant that she didn't have only Archy to fear, but all of the men in his employ. Her nights would be terrifying, to say the least—surely every one of the men had been without women for way too long.

Maggie was now certain that she was the only woman at this ranch!

Chapter 7

How art thou lost! how on a sudden lost,
Defaced, deflowered, and now to death devote!
—John Milton

Sitting tall in his saddle, his red hair standing out against the backdrop of purple alfalfa, Red stared in awe. Until now, he had thought this land was all wilderness and Indians.

He had seen small farms that people had homesteaded, but they were very few and far between. Everyone knew the daily threat that came with living where Indians could sweep down and burn their homes, slaughter their livestock, and kill or take the white people hostages.

But this homestead was vast. It was hard to imagine just how many longhorns he was seeing. Those closest to the ranch house were fenced in, while the others were allowed to roam free. Armed cowhands were posted at what might be critical places, keeping watch in case one of the animals decided to break free.

The ranch house was a long and sprawling place made of cedar logs. It had a wide porch that ran along the front, where two rocking chairs slowly rocked in the morning's gentle breeze. Flowers were blooming in wooden boxes, as though whoever lived there had a loving wife who cared about such things.

The bawling of animals was filled with what sounded like pain. His spine stiffened when, from a distance, he recognized the orange glow of a hot branding iron as one man placed it on the animal while others held it down.

He looked around, seeing a bunkhouse, though no men were near it. They were all working. He saw men everywhere doing their morning chores.

The men's hands went immediately to their holstered pistols as they saw Red and the others ride up on horseback. Red expected some of them to go to their horses to meet their visitors. Everyone he had met on the trail was suspicious of him and his friends when they separated themselves from the wagon train to scout ahead for a waiting Indian ambush. But this morning, Red and the others were allowed to ride toward the ranch house uninterrupted. The cowboys knew that Red and his few men were no threat since there were so many more of the cowhands to stop any trouble they might have in mind.

One of Red's friends, Dave, sidled his horse closer to Red's. "Red, I wonder if this house is that man's who jawed with us for a while yesterday," Dave said, his steely gray eyes cautiously looking around him. "Lord, if it is, he's much richer than I'd have guessed. Look at those longhorns. Look at how many men he has working for him. How does he manage to keep them all alive while living on land that the Indians still consider theirs?"

"I wondered that yesterday when I saw how he rode alone to meet with us," Red confided. "It seems he has a pact with the devil, or the like."

"Like renegades?" Dave asked.

"Let's not jump the gun, Dave," Red said, glancing over at him. "Let's first see if this *is* Archy's place; then we can speculate. I remember him saying that his wife was dead. I wonder if she planted those flowers in the pots before she died, or if this ranch belongs to another man and his wife."

"Whether or not it's Archy's place, there ain't no doubt that this all belongs to a white man. And he surely has some sort of connection with Indians, or he wouldn't be allowed to live in such grandeur out here so close to Indians." Dave's insides tightened as some men stepped from the bunkhouse with rifles in hand.

"Like I said, let's not speculate," Red said, slowly sliding his hand to his holstered pistol at his side. "Let's take this one thing at a time. The most important thing is my niece. My brother's lookin' down from the heavens depending on me."

Dave nodded, then looked over his shoulder as the other men from the wagon train moved in closer. He saw fear, but mainly mistrust, etched on their faces, especially as they stared at the armed men who were watching them.

Chapter 8

O time, arrest your flight! and you,
propitious hours, arrest your
Course! Let us savor the fleeting
delights of our most beautiful days!
                    —Alphonse de Lamartine

Maggie was relieved that the noon meal was behind her, but she still had the evening meal ahead of her before she could have any time to herself. She was looking forward to a bath in the privacy of her room. The copper tub was waiting there now for her.

She would heat the water a teakettle at a time on the cookstove in the kitchen, then carry it to her room until the tub was filled enough for her to hide most of her body beneath the water. She hated it that there was no inside lock on the bedroom door and that Archy could walk in on her at any moment. At night she would sleep with one eye open.

Steam spiraled up from the water she poured into the washbasin in the kitchen. Maggie carried a huge stack of soiled plates over to the counter and set them down. Testing the water she had heated on the cooking stove to make sure it was cool enough, Maggie sank a bar of soap into the water and splashed it around until enough suds were created for her to wash the grubby dishes.

As she began washing one plate after another, she became lost in thought. She had not been disappointing to Archy or any of the men under his employ. And she especially didn't disappoint the two children whose eyes widened when they saw the huge plate of food that Maggie set before them in the privacy of the huge dining room where they ate away from the foul-mouthed, filthy cowhands.

She had waited after giving the children their plates before going back to feed the men. She wanted to see if the children liked what she had prepared for them. She smiled as she recalled how they dove into the food and ate it with big mouthfuls, drinking huge gulps of milk between some of the bites.

At least by seeing to the children's needs, she was doing something worthwhile while being held hostage by the rich cattle baron. The children had not only been starved for affection, but also good food. Cookie had known only how to cook the sort of grub men ate out on the range.

Maggie had returned to the kitchen and the dreaded chore of seeing that the cowhands were fed before beginning their afternoon chores. She shivered at the thought of their crudeness. After she rang the large dinner bell, the men had rushed to the long, narrow room bare of everything except a long table with benches on either side and straight-backed chairs at each end.

Before they sat at the table, they had crowded around a long wooden basin where they took turns working a small, short-handled pump for water. The impatient ones dove their hands into the buckets of water that sat beside the basin, sputtering as they dashed water on their faces and in their hair. Empty flour sacks had served as towels.

She had never seen such grimy hands and dusty faces.

She noticed that some of the men cared more about their appearance than others. They stood before two smoky mirrors in gilt frames that were conveniently placed, below which were a comb and a brush, each suspended on a light brass chain. These men actually primped as they combed or brushed their dust-laden hair to perfection.

Then the men rushed to the benches and plopped down. They attacked the food, shouting "Pass the spuds my way," as the dishes of food made their way around the table.

Some washed this down with steaming hot coffee. Some swallowed huge gulps of milk that Cookie had just brought in from the barn where two dairy cows were kept for such things as milk and freshly churned butter.

Maggie could not help but be proud of what she had accomplished without as much trouble as she had originally thought.

She had prepared fried beefsteaks and boiled potatoes with skins on them and a tall pan of brown gravy. They had gobbled down her large, hot yeast-bread biscuits and emptied a huge steaming kettle of boiled beans. They had drank down several tall pitchers of milk.

Then, much to their delight, she had brought out four pies that she had made from the apples she had found in the fruit cellar beneath the kitchen floor. The men had almost grabbed the pies from the sideboard before she had the chance to slice them.

All in all, she was proud of what she had prepared. She would have never guessed that she could cook for this many men.

She continued dunking plates into the sudsy water, then dipping them into a basin of rinse water, before stacking them to dry.

Suddenly, there was a commotion just outside of the open kitchen window directly in front of where she was washing the dishes. A man came panting, shouting Archy's name. She stood on tiptoe to get a better look from the window. Her heart skipped a beat when she almost came face-to-face with Archy. He stood in the shade of the porch roof, idly smoking a cigar. He was apparently observing the activity around him.

Maggie's heart pounded as she heard a cowhand named Pokey run up to the porch. Redfaced and panting, he stopped directly in front of Archy.

"Strangers are approaching!" Pokey said breathlessly. "See them coming yonder? It might be the woman's kin."

"Do you think I'm blind?" Archy growled out. "I see them. I've got time to get her hid. I'd like to see for myself, first, if it is Maggie's uncle Red. Then I'll know what to do about the situation."

"Archy, do you think all of the cowhands will keep quiet about the woman bein' here?" Pokey asked, looking up and frowning when he saw Maggie looking and listening from the window. "I know everyone agreed to keep quiet in order to have decent food cooked by the woman. But . . ."

"No buts are needed here, Pokey," Archy grumbled. "Everyone knows that I'll kill anyone who doesn't keep their mouth shut. They wouldn't dare tell what I've done, now would they?"

"No, don't think so," Pokey said, swallowing hard.

"Pokey, go and meet the gents and lead 'em on to my house," Archy said.

He turned and gave Maggie a sly smile across his shoulder, then gazed intensely into Pokey's dark eyes again.

"Act friendly, Pokey," he flatly ordered. "We don't want to arouse any suspicions, now do we?"

"What about Maggie?" Pokey asked, looking at her through the window.

"I've got that problem figured out," Archy said. "Now git. Take care of this for me."

Maggie's heart throbbed inside her chest. Her face was flushed with excitement as she saw Red coming with several other men from the wagon train. They were still too far away to see her waving from the window. She had to get outside and run to them, or she might never get the chance again!

Wiping her hands on the apron, her pulse racing, she ran to the kitchen door. But just as she opened it, Archy was there with a cruel grin on his face.

"Goin' somewhere?" he asked in a taunting fashion.

Maggie's jaw tightened. She gave him a shove and tried to run past him, but his strong arm snaked around her waist and quickly stopped her.

"You ain't goin' anywhere but the cellar," Archy said as he yanked her back into the kitchen.

"No!" Maggie cried as she tried to wrench herself free of his steely arm. "I'm not going anywhere with you. Let me go! I want to go to my uncle! I promise not to tell him that you abducted me. I'll . . . lie . . . and say that I wandered off and that . . . that . . . you found me and saved me. I'll tell him that you planned to take me to him today after I got the men fed since they are starved for decent food."

"Just shut up all of that rambling," Archy said, shoving her past him, toward the hidden trapdoor that led down into the fruit cellar.

He managed to hold her by the wrist as he shoved the worktable aside and kicked the rug free of the trapdoor.

"I won't go with you!" Maggie screamed, then winced with pain as his hand tightened around her wrist.

He turned to her and glared into her face. "If I have to warn you one more time about bein' quiet, I'll take the razor strop to you, do you hear?" he gritted out past clenched teeth. "Don't think I won't do it. I use it on my kids when they are disobedient, as well as any man that crosses me."

She was abhorred into silence by the thought of him beating his children. Scarring her flesh with such a thing almost sickened her. She had no choice but to do as he ordered.

"Good," Archy said, a smile quivering across his lips. "You've finally come to your senses. Now cooperate some more, do you hear, as I open the trapdoor? Go willingly or I'll shove you down the stairs. You could end up with a broken leg or arm, or a skull fracture, if you hit that floor hard enough."

Maggie trembled with fear as she waited for him to get the door fully open. Her knees hardly held her up, as he forced her down the rickety steps.

When she reached the cold earthen floor, he quickly tied her hands behind her and gagged her, then shoved her down. He slung a rope around her waist and tied her to a post.

"Now all I need to do is send a certain uncle packing, without his pretty niece," Archy said, laughing menacingly. "Bye, bye, pretty thing. I'll come and get you later, after it's safe to."

Tears filled Maggie's eyes when he closed the trapdoor overhead, leaving her alone, cold, and at the mercy of the spiders and snakes that had managed to make their home among the jars of canned foods and baskets of fruits and vegetables.

From overhead she heard Archy talking to his children, telling them what he had done to Maggie and why. When they began sobbing frantically, he told them to go to their bedroom and stay there until the strangers were gone.

"Why, Pa?" Kevin asked between sobs. "What have you done wrong this time?"

She heard Kevin say, "Pa, you brought this woman here against her will, didn't you?"

Maggie winced when she heard the identifiable sound of a slap, then the cry of pain from the child.

"You be quiet, do you hear?" Archy warned. "Don't you say a word when the men get here. Go now. Take your little brother to your bedroom. Stay there until I say it's okay to come out."

Maggie could imagine Kevin taking Jeremy by the hand, hearing the patter of their bare feet as they hurried to their bedroom and closed the door behind them. She could envision them standing together clinging and crying.

She knew that they were just as much a prisoner of their father as she was, and hoped to find a way to make it better for all of them.

She closed her eyes and began praying that her uncle would guess the truth, and that he was safely trying to remedy her situation.

Chapter 9

The ruling passion, be it what it will,
The ruling passion conquers reason still.
                                    —Alexander Pope

Just as Archy stepped out onto his porch, Red and the other men rode up and stopped a few feet away.

"What can I do for you fellas today?" Archy asked, trying to look guilt free as he forced a broad smile. "What cha doin' away from the wagon train? I thought you'd be long gone by now. What's delayin' your journey on to Oregon?"

"My niece," Red said, looking suspiciously at Archy's unduly flushed face. Red could see the nervous heartbeat in the vein that ran up the side of Archy's neck. "My niece is missing. I expect it's Indians. I need help finding who's responsible for my niece's disappearance."

Red leaned forward and gazed intensely

into Archy's squinty eyes. "Archy, I feel lucky that I found your ranch. Would you and some of your men accompany us? Together we might show enough strength to convince whoever has my niece to hand her over to me."

Red pulled the two pieces of broken arrow from his saddlebag. He held them out for Archy to see. "This was left in my niece's wagon. Whoever it belongs to is the one responsible for my niece's abduction."

Archy pretended to be genuinely sorry about Maggie, while inside he was laughing at how clever he had been. He stepped down from the porch and took the two pieces of arrow.

"I recognize this arrow," he said, giving Red a quick glance. "The Cheyenne carry these in their quivers. I imagine it was Wind Walker. Do you remember if he gave her more attention than he gave the other women when he was among your people?"

"No more than you gave her," Red said, his jaw tight. "But what man wouldn't give my niece a second look? She's as pretty as a picture."

"But remember that we're talkin' about Indians here," Archy replied. "They ain't human, you know, with no human emotion. If they see somethin' they like, they take it."

"But Wind Walker seemed genuinely

friendly," Red softly argued. "I didn't feel
threatened one iota in his presence. Nor did
anyone else. Surely you are wrong to think
Wind Walker did this."

"The arrow is proof enough, ain't it?" Archy
said, his eyes gleaming. "Let me tell you something, Red. Wind Walker is good at pretending
to be friendly. But he is an enemy to all whites.
I keep men posted around my strip of land. I
don't take any chances with that Cheyenne
warrior."

Archy handed the two pieces of the arrow
back to Red. "If you want my suggestion, I'd
say forget Maggie," he said flatly. "She's the
same as dead if she's been taken by *any* Indian."

"No one should give up that quickly on a
loved one," Red argued. "I certainly won't. I
plan to go on to the Cheyenne village. Would
you and some of your men ride with us so that
we can make a larger showing? I have to do all
that I can to find my niece."

Archy slid his hands into his front breeches
pockets. "Well, now, you've come at a bad time
for me," he said. "All of my men are pretty tied
up today, and I have to keep a close watch to
make sure they keep busy. So, no, I'm sorry, but
I can't offer any help, 'cept to draw a map
that'll lead you to the Cheyenne village."

It took all the willpower that Red had within

himself not to get off his horse and hit Archy for his cowardice. But Red would take whatever help he could get. If a map drawn in the dirt was all that he could get from Archy, so be it. For now, at least . . .

He and Dave dismounted. Both knelt down as Archy took up a stick and drew the map that he had promised to show Red.

"Just follow those directions and you'll find yourself at the Cheyenne village before night falls," Archy said, tossing the stick over his shoulder, then pushing himself up from the ground.

After memorizing the map, Red and Dave mounted again. Finding another reason to dislike this abrasive, unfriendly cattle baron, Red sarcastically gave Archy a half salute, then wheeled his horse around and rode away with his men.

Archy chuckled beneath his breath and watched until he couldn't see Red any longer. He turned and hurried to the cellar and released Maggie. He forced her to her bedroom, then he closed the door.

"Now you are mine. Your uncle left without you. It's time for a little play, Maggie," he said, his eyes gleaming into hers. "Take off your clothes. I've waited long enough to get a taste of that sweet flesh."

Maggie went cold inside. She had known

this would eventually happen. An amoral man such as Archy could not refrain from being the animal he was.

She quickly tried to think of something that would dissuade him, at least for a little while, which might give her time to escape. "Can we come to an agreement . . . make a bargain?" she ventured. "I will be good to your children and continue to cook and clean for you, and make all of the meals for the men—but only if you will leave me alone."

He let out a loud, mocking laugh, then grabbed her by the shoulders as he spoke into her face. "You foolish woman. Don't you know that you are in no position to bargain?"

"You're wrong," Maggie said, trying to keep him from seeing how frightened she was. "I can refuse to treat your children decently. I can cook terrible meals for your men. I could put soap in the food. I hope you have enough room in your outhouse for all of them to be there at one time."

"There's nothing you can say that will stop me from getting what I want from you *now*, not later," he said tightly. "I'll remind you again about the razor strop. And then there is the fruit cellar. I could lock you down there for a full night. And you aren't the sort to treat children badly."

Tears filled Maggie's eyes. "I have never

been with a man before," she said, sobbing. "Please don't take my virginity from me. And . . . and . . . I'm having my monthly flow. Surely you won't force yourself on me in that condition."

She placed a hand to her brow. "I'm feeling ill," she murmured. "Working so hard on my feet today has given me terrible belly cramps. I need to rest, at least for a little while. Please?"

Archy took a step away from her. His eyes wavered. "Well, all right," he said. "But only for a couple of days. Then, by God, I will have a piece of you, and to hell with you bein' a virgin."

"Thank you," Maggie said, glad to have a little more time to find a way to escape.

"Go and bathe my kids, and then you can rest," Archy said, opening the door and gesturing toward it. "Git. Suddenly I've lost my appetite for you."

Maggie slid past him, then went to the children's bedroom. Soon both boys were sitting together in a copper tub filled with warm water. As they bathed each other, Maggie found a clean change of clothes for them in a trunk at the foot of their bed. She returned and sat down on the floor beside the tub as they washed.

Kevin suddenly opened up to her. "You've got to find a way to get away from here," he said, soap shining on his chest. "My father is cruel to women. Our mother died because Pa beat her so often. Eventually he will beat you, too. *You* might die."

Panic grabbed at Maggie's insides. She knew she had to find a way to get out of this mess. But she now realized how important it was to get the children away, as well. But how?

She held a towel up so that Kevin could climb from the tub behind it; then Maggie wrapped it around him and did the same for Jeremy. She gathered them around her and hugged them. They both seemed hungry for her embrace.

She felt sorry for the children, but she was in no position to help them. She couldn't even help herself.

Bone weary, she left them alone to dress and went to her own room. She knew that she had left the dishes half-done, but for now, the only important thing was to stretch out and rest, and to think.

She had looked forward to finding a reprieve from her endless day when she could climb onto the bed's soft feather mattress. Maggie stretched out and imagined being with the wagon train again, sitting beside a large campfire, as one of the men played a zither harp. She had enjoyed the sudden enlivening strains of "Turkey in the Straw."

But all she could hear now was the bellowing of the longhorns and the shouts of the men at work. She opened her eyes and looked determinedly at the lovely blue sky through the window.

Somehow, some way, she *would* leave this horrid place . . . with the children.

Chapter 10

The sacred fruit forbidden!
Some cursed fraud
Of enemy hath beguiled thee!
—John Milton

As dusk fell, Red saw the Indian village through a break in the trees. Its many tepees sat back from a river, smoke spiraling lazily from their smoke holes. Children romped and played. Elderly men sat back from an outdoor fire that had been built in the center of the village. Horses were penned in corrals behind the lodges.

His eyes fell on a much larger tepee that sat amidst the others, which he surmised was either the chief's lodge or the Cheyenne's council house.

His gaze was drawn to a beautiful woman coming from the river with a jug of water. She walked gracefully with pride in each step. Her long braids fell down her back. Her copper face had beautiful, dainty features.

An ache circled his heart as a child ran up to the woman and grabbed her by a hand. His face was radiant with love as he looked up at the woman and talked anxiously to her. This was obviously a mother and child.

Red saw a scene of peace, harmony, and love. He remembered the somber, hideous tales of soldiers going into Indian villages, slaughtering without question.

"Red, we're almost there," Dave said as he sidled his horse closer to Red's. "Should we stop and study the surroundings before entering? Who is to say how we will be accepted among the Cheyenne? If they have themselves a white captive, they won't allow us anywhere near their village."

Red drew his steed to a halt. "You are jumping to too many conclusions," he grumbled, although fear grabbed at his insides. He *was* near an Indian village, where surely white people were greatly resented.

He knew that he and the other men could be breathing their last breaths if Wind Walker *was* an enemy. But he must risk his life—if that's what it took—in order to see if Maggie was there.

"It's just that now that I think about it, I think it's foolish to have come here without the assistance of the cavalry," Dave said, his eyes wide with fear. "Maybe we should turn back. . . ."

"No, we're not going to turn back like yellow-bellied cowards," Red said flatly.

He looked over his shoulder at the other men, who had not offered their opinions. They looked as frightened as Dave.

"If you don't want to go with me, say so now," Red said, his voice drawn. "I understand how you're feeling. I'm just as afraid as the rest of you. But . . . we've got to do what we can to save Maggie. She doesn't deserve to be forgotten."

The men nodded in unison. "We're with you all of the way," one of them said. "Come on. What are we waiting for?"

Red gave them a warm smile, then turned to Dave. "And you?" he asked. "Are you with us? Or do you want to return to the camp? It's up to you. No one is going to stop you."

"I'll stay," Dave said, looking almost humbly at Red. "Sorry for causing you trouble when you have too much stress as it is. Let's go."

They turned to continue onward, but stopped when they saw a warrior leave the village on horseback, riding directly toward them. When the warrior got close enough for Red to see his features, he quickly recognized him. It was Blue Wing, the warrior who had been Wind Walker's companion yesterday.

Red saw no trace of anger or resentment on Blue Wing's face or in his dark eyes. If the

Cheyenne had anything to hide, surely they would have sent warriors out to meet the strangers approaching their village. Their show of force would frighten any white man away.

But Blue Wing smiled and placed a fist over his heart, which Red assumed was a friendly gesture.

Blue Wing rode on up to him and stopped. "You are the white men from the wagon train," he said. He looked from one to the other, then centered his attention on Red, who seemed to be the leader of the group, as he had been the spokesperson for them yesterday.

"Yes, and as you and Wind Walker came to us yesterday, we come to you in peace today," Red said. He reached a hand out for a handshake.

Understanding this offer of friendship, Blue Wing accepted it and shook hands with Red.

"What brings you here to my people's village?" Blue Wing asked.

"My niece, my Maggie," Red said. "Someone came in the night and abducted her from her wagon. We came today to seek your help. Could you please help us find her? You might remember her. She was the woman who sat next to me. Her hair is the same color as mine."

Red didn't see anything unusual about Blue Wing's reaction to his tale. Concern showed in his dark eyes. Suddenly, Red knew that his niece had not been abducted by this clan of Cheyenne.

"Come and have council," Blue Wing said, nodding toward his village. "Our warriors are already in the council house, having smoke and food. Come. You can share with us as we talk about your niece."

"Thank you," Red said, almost choked up over the generous nature of the Indian.

In truth, considering the horror stories of the white cavalrymen, this Indian should resent Red and his friends. He should run them off and tell them not to show their face anywhere near his village again. But instead, he trusted that Red spoke the truth and was ready to offer assistance.

Blue Wing led the way into his village. Everything seemed to stop all around him. The children grew quiet and still, the elderly guardedly watched.

But Blue Wing continued to lead Red and his men through the village, stopping only when he reached the larger tepee. Blue Wing dismounted. A young brave ran to him and took his reins.

Blue Wing walked up beside Red's horse, then looked at the others. "All of you, dismount and your steeds will be seen to."

The men followed Red's lead as he swung

himself out of his saddle and handed his reins to another young brave. Red saw a look of mistrust in some of his men's eyes, as though they thought they might be seeing their steeds for the last time, but they walked away with Red and Blue Wing, into the large tepee. Many warriors were sitting around a fire, food in wooden platters before them.

Wind Walker turned when he heard the arriving footsteps. When he saw Blue Wing entering with several white men, he got quickly to his feet and greeted them.

"As I was coming to the council house I saw the white men approaching our village," Blue Wing said, gazing over his shoulder at the men. He turned to Wind Walker again. "They need our help. A woman is missing. She was taken in the night."

Wind Walker recalled how one particular white woman had affected him. He could feel it even now. Their eyes had met and held, and he had felt something for a woman for the first time since the death of his wife.

Of course he did not like it that a white woman had caused these feelings, but she had. There was no denying it, nor was there any way around it.

Red stepped up to Wind Walker. "My niece, Maggie, the woman who sat beside me when you visited us at the wagon train. She was

taken from her wagon some time in the night,"
he said. He held the broken arrow up for Wind
Walker to see. "Whoever abducted her left this
in her wagon. I imagine it broke as . . . as . . . he
wrestled with her."

Wind Walker was startled by the news.
Someone had taken the beautiful woman. His
jaw tightened.

"An arrow of my people's markings," he
said, eyeing the arrow, trying hard not to react.

He frowned at Red. "Yes, this is from my
people's weapons, but we did not abduct your
woman," he said. "It was placed there to throw
suspicion on us."

"I figured that," Red said, nodding. He took
the pieces of arrow back from Wind Walker. "I
remembered how sincere you were yesterday. I
could not imagine you taking an innocent
woman as your captive."

Wind Walker smiled. "It is good that you felt
the kindness I offered you. Come and sit with
me and my friends," he said, gesturing toward
the circle of warriors. Their eyes had not left
the white men since they had entered their
council lodge. "Share food and smoke with us.
Then we can talk over who I think might be responsible for having done this."

"I shall never forget your generosity," Red
said, swallowing hard. He nodded over his
shoulder at the men who were with him, and

they followed him as he sat down among the warriors.

Red leaned toward the fire and tossed the broken arrow into the flames. It was useless. It had been used to cast blame where it should not be cast.

Red hoped that Wind Walker knew the land and its people well enough to figure out who had Maggie. Red could not help but think of Archy and his arrogance upon Red's arrival at his ranch. Nor could he forget how uncooperative he had been by not offering to help in the search.

Wind Walker took a pipe from where it had been wrapped in its special bundle of purifying sagebrush. He filled the red stone bowl with his people's special tobacco and went over in his mind what Red had said.

Red and his men had gone to Archy's ranch, and after showing Archy the broken arrow, he had purposely led the white men astray. He knew that neither Wind Walker, nor any of the warriors of his clan, would abduct a white woman. That was not the sort of thing they did.

Wind Walker was mildly surprised by the cattle baron's behavior. He had never trusted Archy. And now Wind Walker had proof why he shouldn't. Archy had purposely lied to Red.

Wind Walker had always suspected an alliance between the renegade Utes and Archy. He might have made a wrong move today. If he would take a white woman captive, Wind Walker believed that Archy was capable of anything.

Realizing that he was spending too much time in thought, Wind Walker handed the lit pipe to his left, where Red sat with his legs crossed before him.

"The bowl of this pipe represents the earth," Wind Walker said as Red gingerly took the pipe in his hand. "The wooden stem represents all that grows upon this earth. The twelve feathers that hang from the stem represent all winged things of the air. Inhale smoke from the pipe. By doing so our friendship is strengthened. When you are finished taking a smoke, send it on to your left. It will make its way around the circle until it returns to me. Then I, too, will smoke from it before returning it to its special bundle of sagebrush."

Red inhaled, tasting something sweet, yet bitter, then passed it to Dave, at his left. It passed around as everyone watched and sat in silence. Finally it returned to Wind Walker's hand, and he took the last smoke. Then platters of baked buffalo meat, chokeberries, and honey were passed around.

After everyone was comfortably full, Wind Walker folded his arms across his bare chest and gazed over at Red. He didn't say what he was thinking, that if renegades had come to the wagon train in the night, they would not take only a woman. They would have left death and destruction behind.

This was the work of someone else—Archy.

Archy was as mean and as untrustworthy as a snake. And Archy was not the sort of man to go out of his way to a wagon train unless it benefited him.

Had he seen the woman and wanted her? *Hee-hec*, yes. The coward that he was, Archy was more than likely to steal a woman like a thief in the night. This was something that Wind Walker would need to look into.

"Red, I urge you not to go farther with the search. You will find only death, not your niece," Wind Walker said, causing surprise to leap into the white man's eyes. "I strongly urge you to let Cheyenne warriors search for and find your niece. We are more familiar with the land and the people who inhabit it. We would have a better chance of finding her without lives being taken. I believe I know who is responsible. Be patient. Allow me and my warriors to see if my conclusions are right. If so, you will have your niece with you again very soon. I, personally, will see to that."

"How can you ask that of me?" Red asked. "I can't just sit around waiting for her to be returned to me. I want her to see my face the moment she is rescued. She might think that you have rescued her only to have her for yourself."

"I will reassure her that is not my reason," Wind Walker said, his jaw tight. "Trust me. I speak in fluent English. I will speak to her and make her understand that I am doing this for her uncle. If you accompany us, you will only slow us down. We have our own way of doing things. You would only be in the way."

"If I don't accompany you, when will you look for her?" Red asked, his voice drawn.

"I need time, but I cannot say exactly how much," Wind Walker said. "Let us make a pact. Give me the time I need and if I do not find your niece, I will come to you and we can join forces for a further search. Go now back to your camp. Stay there. You will be safer if you show strength by numbers should renegades come to ambush you."

Red looked up at the sky. "It's almost dark. It will take some time for us to return to our camp. Is it safe to travel at night?"

"With some of my warriors riding as escort, it is," Wind Walker said, nodding. He placed a hand on Red's shoulder. "And so you agree to my plan? You will allow me to search for your niece?"

"Yes. It's a bargain. I believe that you are

right. Please do what you can," Red said somberly. "If you find her, I will forever be grateful."

They clasped hands to seal the pact, then Wind Walker moved to his feet. "Go now. Your trust is appreciated."

He looked around his circle of men and called the names of those who would accompany Red back to his camp. Together they left the council house.

As Red waited for his and the other horses to be brought from the corral, he studied Wind Walker. He hoped that he was not being deceived. Such a deception would cost him not only his life, but also his niece's and everyone else at the wagon train!

Chapter 11

Bright eyes, accomplish'd shape,
And lang'rous waist!
—John Keats

Wind Walker rode through rolling sagebrush country with low hills all about him. Russian thistles rolled past him. The tumbleweeds lived up to their name. Whenever a wind stirred them, they rolled and jumped and went a great distance, scattering their foul, despised seeds everywhere. They had the ability to take root almost anywhere.

Wind Walker scared a sleepy, long-eared jackrabbit that hopped away with a great burst of speed. He didn't pay attention to the jackrabbit or the rolling sagebrush. He was focused on one thing today. He was going to Archy's ranch to see if there were any signs of the white woman. If Maggie was there, he was adamant about rescuing her.

He rode steadily onward. The sun hung low in the west now, soon to be replaced by the moon and stars in the sky. It was his plan to arrive at the ranch before dark. He wanted to have enough time to study the activity at the ranch. If luck was with him, if Maggie was there, he would get a glimpse of her.

He had already worked it out in his mind how he would rescue her, and he would make certain nothing and no one stopped him.

He heard a loud bellowing sound. Looking far to the left, Wind Walker saw many longhorned beasts grazing amidst the purple alfalfa. His jaw tightened. The man who owned them had changed the landscape he homesteaded.

The animals from his home in Texas were the worst. They grazed over a huge piece of land that had, until recently, belonged solely to the red man.

Now white settlers came, taking everything they saw, especially the buffalo. The large herds were dwindling down now to almost nothing and longhorn cattle grazed on the land.

The Cheyenne were the great buffalo hunters of the northern plains. Though it caused an ache inside his belly that the white man had taken the buffalo, it made him proud that nothing and no one could take away the Cheyenne dignity and nobility.

When he came to within sight of the ranch, he sought shelter amidst a thick stand of cottonwood and box elder trees that grew along a creek.

He dismounted and hobbled his horse near a bush, where he knelt down and readied himself for what might be a long night of watching and waiting. But his patience was his virtue.

The sun continued its descent in the sky as time passed slowly. The rumbling in Wind Walker's stomach made him aware that his evening mealtime had passed. He went quietly to his horse and reached inside his rawhide parfleche bag and took a pemmican cake from those he had packed.

His mother had taught him to make pemmican, the all-purpose emergency food of the plains. It was nutritious and would keep for many years in storage. It was made by mixing dried buffalo meat, boiled fat, and chokeberries. She taught him to use a large stone hammer to pound the meat until it was nearly powder and the bones to boil out the fat.

Focusing his mind back on the duty at hand, his dark eyes watched the movement outside the ranch house and the bunkhouse.

He tried to see into the windows of the main house, but the lowering sun, burning an orange-red, was casting its light onto the panes of glass.

His eyes widened and his spine stiffened as Maggie appeared at the side door of the house, holding a bucket.

He watched with an anxious heartbeat, wishing he could mount his steed, ride up, and take her away.

She stood there for a moment, then tossed water from the bucket to settle in pools on the ground. She lingered, entranced by the loveliness of the sunset.

Suddenly a hand reached out and grabbed her by an arm, the empty bucket falling to the ground, as Maggie was yanked back inside the house. The door slammed shut behind her.

"Archy," Wind Walker grumbled to himself. His eyes narrowed angrily as he tried to look through the windows, but the sun was still reflecting in them. He couldn't see anything.

He waited as day turned to night, his eyes never leaving the house. Lamplight suddenly appeared in some of the windows. His mouth went dry when he saw Maggie in one of the front windows at the far end of the house.

She stopped and stared out into the night, her face illuminated in lamplight. His pulse raced as he saw again how beautiful she was.

She raised the windowpane to let in the sweet night air, but she did not attempt to leave through it. Archy had probably warned her that she was being watched.

But Wind Walker knew how to silence sentries, at least for the length of time he needed to get the woman through the window and take her away. But still, he had to wait for the right opportunity.

He watched and waited as one by one the light was extinguished at each window. His heart pounded rapidly inside his chest as he stared at the window where he had seen Maggie. Her lamp was out, but the window remained open.

Through the moonlit night, he saw that no one stood near Maggie's window. It puzzled him. Wind Walker scanned the area further. His eyes stopped on a man standing against a tree, his head hung, looking as though he was sound asleep.

Another man stood in the shadows, but he too slept, his back resting against the wall of the bunkhouse.

Wind Walker would take no chances, however. His eyes searched around him until he found a nice-size rock, one that could knock someone out in one blow.

He waited until he could be sure Maggie was asleep. Wind Walker feared that if she saw a red man climbing through her bedroom window, her first instinct would be to scream.

He waited patiently for a while longer, then sprang lithely to his feet. He unsnapped the buckskin sheath, slid his sharp knife out. Then, with the rock in one hand and his knife in his other, he ran from the cover of the bushes. His eyes moved steadily from place to place; his moccasined feet were silent as a panther's as he moved toward the house.

He moved like an animal hunkered low to the ground, getting past one sentry, then disabling the other with a blow to the head.

As he ran, Wind Walker kept his knife ready should he be forced to use it.

Finally he was standing just outside the room where Maggie was being held captive. He dropped the rock. His heart beat like great claps of thunder as he waited for his breathing to slow down. He sucked in a wild breath and turned quickly to climb through the window.

Wind Walker found himself standing over Maggie's bed. The moon's glow revealed her sleeping soundly in her nightgown, her long hair around the pillow like a red halo. Her thick lashes rested on her pink cheeks, and her lips parted.

The temptation to bend low and kiss her was almost too much to bear. But he reminded himself to finish the mission safely.

Hoping not to frighten her too much, Wind Walker slid the knife back inside his sheath. He bent low over Maggie and clasped a hand over her mouth.

She quickly awoke, and in the moonlight, Wind Walker saw fear in her eyes.

"You know me as a friend," he whispered to her. "I have come to rescue you."

Maggie tried to yank his hand from her mouth, remembering the last time a man silenced her the same way.

"Please believe me when I say that I come in friendship," Wind Walker said as he fought against her fingers pulling at his hand. "I am Wind Walker. I have come tonight to rescue you. Your uncle Red and I made a pact. I have sworn to find you for him. I know the evil Archy is capable of. When I heard that you were abducted, I immediately thought of him. Trust me. You will not regret it."

He hated seeing her fear. But defiance shone in her eyes, as though she didn't believe or trust him. There was not much else he could do to reassure her. She probably wouldn't believe him until he handed her over to her uncle.

Maggie's heart was pounding inside her chest. Just before she went to sleep, she had been thinking about this Indian, and now here he was. He vowed he came in the dark to rescue her. He said that he had made a pact with her uncle. What was she to believe?

But now, all that she could think about was getting away from this place, and he was offering her freedom. She could only hope that he was telling the truth.

Maggie remembered how he and his friend came to the wagon train to warn them about the renegades. She had heard the kindness in his voice and seen it in his eyes.

Yes, he was the sort of man her uncle would go to for help, even if his skin was red. She listened to her heart—a heart that suddenly believed and trusted.

She knew she had to get away from Archy and his men. But what of the children? She had hoped to find a way to take them away from this hell on earth.

Maggie realized she had to consider herself for now. She would find a way to come back for the children.

She stopped struggling and lowered her hands to her sides. She nodded to Wind Walker.

He saw Maggie's sudden agreement. Yet he still didn't trust her enough to take his hand from her mouth, not until he was far from the dangers of this ranch.

As he started to take her out through the window, she mumbled something behind his hand.

Hoping that she wouldn't scream, he slowly slid his hand away. His spine was stiff as he waited for her to speak.

"I won't cry out," she whispered. "Please, take me away from this horrible place." She lowered her eyes, then looked into his. "And thank you."

"I will not let anyone hurt you," he whispered back to her. "Now come. We must be careful. I downed one sentry, but there was another. If we are in luck, he is still asleep."

She nodded, then climbed from the window. He landed softly next to her and offered her a hand. Maggie took it, sliding her palm against his. The warmth of his flesh caused a sensual feeling to sweep through her.

Reminding herself of the immediate danger, she ran with him across the yard. She was panting hard when they safely reached the cover of darkness amidst the tall trees.

A moment of doubt seized her. Was she right to trust Wind Walker?

Feeling Maggie stiffen, Wind Walker placed gentle hands on her shoulders and turned her to face him. Their eyes met and held.

"I am an honest man. I tell the truth," he said. "Your uncle came to me for help. He came to me in the name of friendship. I will take you to my village, where you will be reunited with your uncle."

He slid his hands down and placed them at her waist. Then he turned her toward his horse and lifted her onto its back. Wind Walker mounted behind her. As he slid a protective arm around her waist, he felt her flinch.

"You still doubt me. In time you will believe that I am a man of my word," he said, drawing her eyes to his.

For a moment, their gaze held. She turned away from him as he flicked the reins and they rode off in the direction of his village.

Her red hair fluttered in the wind, teasing Wind Walker's face with its softness. He could not help but be transfixed by her all over again.

Chapter 12

All was gloom, and silent all,
Save now and then the still foot-fall
Of one returning homewards late,
Past the echoing minster-gate.
—John Keats

The world was still shrouded in black as night lingered. Yet there was enough light from the moon's glow for Maggie to see that Wind Walker's village was large, with many skin te-pees. Everyone seemed to be asleep, with slight spirals of smoke rising from the smoke holes.

Maggie started to feel afraid again the far-ther they rode into the village. What if she had been wrong to trust Wind Walker? She would not be able to escape from this place any better than she could have from Archy's.

She had seen several sentries posted at strategic places around the village as she had approached it with Wind Walker. Their eyes had captured his and they nodded in silent ac-knowledgment.

Maggie could not see their reaction to her. It was too dark to see such details in their midnight-dark eyes. But she could not believe that she would be welcomed among the Cheyenne people. She was white and perhaps loathed by most.

"Do not be afraid," Wind Walker said, surprising Maggie as he seemed to read her thoughts. "You are safe among my people. They respect those who respect them."

"But they don't even know me," Maggie whispered. "How can they trust me?"

"They trust me to make the right decisions on who to bring or not to bring among them," Wind Walker softly explained.

He nodded toward a large tepee as he drew a tight rein before it. "This is my home," he said, dismounting.

He reached for Maggie and helped her from the saddle to the ground beside him. She trembled from the cold. Her feet were bare and her nightgown was little protection against the night air. She hugged herself as Wind Walker took his horse to the corral, then came back to her.

"Come inside with me," Wind Walker said as he held his entrance flap aside. "It will be warmer beside my lodge fire."

Still uncertain of whether she should trust him, Maggie paused. Wind Walker waited patiently. Maggie realized she had no other choice but to do as he asked. She hurried past him into the tepee and stopped at the circle of rocks where a fire was barely discernible. But what little warmth there was felt good to her. She stepped closer and held her hands over the heat.

Wind Walker walked around to the other side of the firepit. Red crackling embers cast a faint light upon his long black hair and sculpted copper face. He knelt and lifted one log, then another onto the fire, where flames soon took hold.

Wind Walker watched as Maggie's eyes became transfixed on the fire. She knelt down and held her hands close to the heat. He could not help but allow his eyes to linger on her for a moment longer.

Being alone with her now, he realized just how much he cared for her, as though some unseen force was bringing them together. He could not fight his feelings. She was so lovely. She was petite yet so deliciously curved under the long nightgown that she wore. Her flame-colored hair was brilliant in the firelight. Her features were beautiful and alluring.

He shook himself from his reverie. "It is late," he said, bringing her eyes to him. "You need rest. In the morning, I will see to it that you have warm food and a change of clothes."

Wind Walker stepped back into the dark shadows and brought out only one blanket. Maggie's insides stiffened. She suddenly thought herself a fool for believing him. Surely he had taken her from Archy's clutches for only one reason—to have her for himself.

Wind Walker was keenly aware of how quickly Maggie's attitude changed. Her eyes were flashing into his, yet he was not sure why. He had done nothing wrong. He tried to avoid her steady stare.

Maggie stood up and angrily placed her hands on her hips. Wind Walker lay the blanket aside and got ermine and marten pelts. He stretched them out close to the fire.

"You will find comfort in my bed," Wind Walker said, again picking up the blanket and handing it to her. "The pelts upon which you will sleep are soft. The blanket is warm."

"I see only one bed and only one blanket," Maggie accused. "I shall not share those with you. Never. Do you hear? Never! And I will escape at my first opportunity."

Wind Walker took a quick step away from her, his eyes searching hers. "Do you truly feel threatened by me?" he asked steadily. "Do you truly believe that I would force you into my bed? The pelts and blanket are for your use alone. I will be sleeping outside to ensure your privacy."

He dropped the blanket on top of the pelts. Wind Walker retrieved his own to take outside, then stopped before leaving the lodge and looked at her again.

"Leave if you wish," he said softly. "I will not stop you, nor will the sentries."

He leaned closer to her. "But I must warn you, once you leave, you will find yourself alone in the middle of the night with two- and four-legged creatures that roam Cheyenne land. You might not make it to the morning's sunrise alive."

Maggie's heart skipped a beat. Her eyes wavered and she lowered them. She knew that he was right, and although she thought he might be trying to scare her, she had no choice but to stay.

"I am tired," she murmured, avoiding his eyes. "Thank you for the pelts and blankets."

He said nothing, just turned and went on outside.

After informing his sentries that she was free to leave should she try, Wind Walker stretched out on the ground beside his entrance flap and covered himself with his blanket. But he could not sleep. He kept wondering what Maggie's next move might be. Wind Walker doubted his decision to leave her alone in his tepee with his cache of weapons.

Would she be able to kill anyone? If she truly

believed that he was being devious, Wind Walker didn't know what she was capable of doing. Hoping to find peace in the black void of night, he closed his eyes.

His heart skipped a beat when he heard Maggie crying. He resisted the temptation to go back inside and offer her his arms for comfort. Too much mistrust had been in her eyes and he knew that she would not be ready to let him comfort her.

He forced his eyes closed. He must find solace in sleep. . . .

Chapter 13

Doubt thou the stars are fire,
Doubt that the sun doth move,
Doubt truth to be a liar,
But never doubt I love.
        —William Shakespeare

Maggie snuggled beneath the blanket. She could not deny how wonderful the pelts felt beneath her. They were soft and warm against her body.

But soon she started to think about all that had happened to her. She missed her uncle. And she missed her freedom.

She tossed to one side, then the other, as she tried to sleep.

"I can't believe all of these things keep happening to me," she whispered as tears welled in her eyes.

First her father died suddenly, then her mother, and now this.

She tried to will her eyes to shut. She would deal with everything tomorrow when her mind was fresh. She had always been able to think more clearly at the break of dawn.

But her eyes wouldn't stay closed. Maggie leaned up on an elbow and looked slowly around her. The tepee was huge and spacious, much larger than she had ever envisioned one to be.

Men's buckskin clothing hung from one of the poles that held the tepee in place. The fringed breeches and shirts were decorated with designs in dyed porcupine quills.

Wind Walker's weapons rested near two fine willow rests and a stack of thick, colorful bulrush mats. Lush pelts and blankets were rolled up against one side of the tepee. There were a few wooden plates and eating utensils but no cooking pots.

Thunder growled in the distance causing Maggie's stomach to tighten. She reminded herself that she wasn't in a wagon. She was safe in a tepee.

Maggie began sweating and trembling as the storm got closer to the village. Its ferocity could be felt beneath the mat-covered earth. A clap of thunder caused her to let out a loud scream.

Wind Walker woke with his heart pounding. He rushed from beneath the blanket and hurried into his lodge. He found Maggie sitting up, hugging the blanket around her, her eyes wide. As she gazed up at him through her tears, he hurried to her and knelt before her.

"Are you so afraid of being with me that you would have nightmares?" he asked, his eyes searching hers.

"No," she answered, trembling. "It's the storm. I was never afraid of storms until . . ."

"Until when?" he softly urged.

"I feel so foolish." She sniffed. "I have always been so strong, yet with this . . ."

"You have nothing to fear," Wind Walker said as he was reminded of another storm, another woman. "You are safe."

"I want to feel safe," Maggie said. "But so much has happened."

Wind Walker dared to reach out and embrace her.

At first she stiffened, but soon relaxed into the protection of his arms. Maggie's breath was momentarily stolen as she allowed herself to be comforted by him.

Maggie recalled her first reaction to him. She remembered the moment his eyes held hers filled with soft gentleness. At that moment, she had felt something for a man for the first time in her life.

And now, he was holding her and she was allowing it. She didn't know if it was foolish, but she enjoyed the sensation.

Wind Walker was aware of her abating tears.

He could not help but care for her. One thing was for certain, he did not want to lose this trust. He wanted nothing to stand in the way of what might have begun here tonight.

The storm passed overhead without one raindrop falling. Feeling safe, Maggie eased from Wind Walker's arms. She looked into his eyes and felt herself taken heart and soul by him.

"I . . . I'm all right," she said breathlessly. "Please take me to my uncle tonight."

Suddenly, she needed to put distance between them and her feelings. "Surely it is safe enough to travel now. Soon it will be morning."

"I risked much traveling alone tonight to rescue you from Archy's ranch," he said. "With you on my steed, the dangers were twofold, for a woman is a much sought prize. No. I cannot leave the safety of my village right now. But you will be reunited with your uncle soon. Trust me."

"All right," Maggie relented. "I do understand the danger."

In truth, she felt close to Wind Walker. He had proven that he meant her no harm, but instead, offered protection. She was a stranger, yet she felt important to him.

And he was important to her. She was having feelings for him and hoped that she wasn't wrong to allow them.

Wind Walker quietly got up and left, and Maggie stretched out on the softness of the pelts and drew the blanket over her. She now felt guilty that he had to sleep out in the open, alone, while she took comfort in what surely was his bed.

She lifted a corner on one of the pelts to her nose and inhaled his smell—so manly, yet so clean, like river water. She pressed it against her cheek, smiled, then closed her eyes and drifted off into a peaceful sleep.

Wind Walker pulled the blanket around him as he lay beneath the stars that were now fading in the sky, traces of morning evident behind the distant mountains.

He could not get his mind off Maggie. He smiled as he recalled her willingly coming into his arms and accepting his comfort.

He drifted off into a restful sleep, the smell of Maggie clinging to him like a sweet elixir to his senses.

Chapter 14

Shed no tear—O shed no tear!
The flower will bloom another year.
Weep no more—O weep no more!
　　　　　　　　—John Keats

The sun was just splashing its light along the horizon. Birds were waking in the trees and engaging in their morning chatter. Wind Walker yawned. He had not fully awakened as he lay beneath the blanket on the cold, hard ground.

Someone placed a hand on his arm and spoke his name. His eyes sprang open and he jumped. Sky Dreamer, his people's shaman, knelt beside him.

"Wind Walker, I went to our chief's lodge moments ago to check on his welfare as is my duty," he said. "He was awake. His breathing was labored and he clutched my hand as though in desperation. He asked for you to come to him."

Sky Dreamer momentarily lowered his eyes.

"Our chief says that he dreamed his time is nigh," he said thickly. "Dreams are messages from the spirits."

Still dressed in the buckskins and moccasins that he had worn yesterday, and his hair tangled from his restless night, Wind Walker rushed to his feet. "*Nai-ish*, thank you, for coming for me."

"I shall go on to my lodge," Sky Dreamer said, walking beside Wind Walker as he headed for Chief Half Moon's lodge. "This is your time alone with our chief."

"All time with him is cherished," Wind Walker said. "Who is to know from one moment to the next if it will be the last?"

"*Hee-hec*, that is so." Sky Dreamer slowly nodded.

Sky Dreamer continued walking as Wind Walker stopped at the large tepee of his chief. He shoved the entrance flap aside and went in. Chief Half Moon laid on thick, plush pelts.

The chief made his bed as close to the fire as he could get. His failing health made it difficult to keep warm.

Wind Walker paused before going to his chief. He could not fight back the lump that had appeared in his throat. Each day brought his chief closer to his journey to *Se-han*, the place of the dead. It might even be today.

The chief's breathing was shallow and his

eyes were sunken. His lips lay thin and drawn and strangely twisted, making it almost impossible to see them. Chief Half Moon had brought his blankets up just beneath his chin, obviously trying to keep warm.

Chief Half Moon let out a strange gargling cough that came from deep within his lungs. His eyes flew open from its intensity. Wind Walker went to him, and the chief's eyes lit up when he found his favorite warrior bending over him, filling his muscled arms with him.

"It is good that you came," Half Moon said, wrapping his trembling arms around Wind Walker, the bony fingers of one hand gently patting Wind Walker on the back.

"You know that I am always here for you," Wind Walker answered. He eased from his chief's arms, then sat down beside him. He watched as Half Moon struggled to sit up, only to give up and lay back down on his bed of pelts.

Wind Walker did not offer to help, for he knew that his chief was not strong enough to sit. When he ate, someone held his head slightly tilted as someone else fed him. Nothing solid, only broth now. It seemed so strange to Wind Walker to see such a strong and powerful man rendered helpless. He would give his beloved chief what comfort he could.

"Wind Walker," Chief Half Moon said, as he

slowly turned to one side to gaze at the future chief of his people. "You know that our Golden Eagle Clan of Cheyenne have always prided ourselves in being peacemakers. Remember, when you have sons, if one of them is killed in front of your tepee, you should take a peace pipe and smoke. Then you would be called an honest chief!"

Wind Walker listened again regardless he had heard the same advice from his chief many times before. He leaned forward as his chief struggled to remember. Half Moon's old eyes squinted and his lips grew tight, into a thin, narrow line. Finally, his eyes lit up as he grasped on to what he wanted to say. "If ever war is needed, remember that chiefs own the land and people. If your warriors retreat from the fight, *you* are not to step back, but take a stand to protect your land and people."

Half Moon closed his eyes and licked his lips, then gazed into Wind Walker's eyes once again. "My most prized warrior of all," he said, true pride in his trembling voice. "Always take time to be among your people and talk to them. It is important that they feel important."

As Half Moon continued giving advice, Wind Walker sat attentive, nodding and smiling at the right times.

"Remember, too, that when you meet someone, or he comes to your tepee and asks for

anything, give it to him," Half Moon said.
"Never refuse. Then go outside to sing your
chief's song so that all people will know that
you have done something admirable."

Half Moon reached out and took Wind
Walker's hand in his. "My *ne-ha*, son, it is time
for the Massaum of Crazy Lodge Ceremony for
this old chief. Will you make the preparations
for me? It needs to be done soon, Wind Walker,
if it is ever to be done at all."

"I shall prepare everything for you with
haste," Wind Walker said somberly.

"*Nai-ish*, thank you," Half Moon said, sighing heavily. "But first take me to the river
where I can sing my song of death."

Wind Walker felt as though his heart were
going to break. To sing one's song was to welcome death. Half Moon was ready to reunite
with those who had gone before him. Half
Moon's devoted wife slipped away into the
night some moons ago and traveled to *Se-han*,
where she now awaited the arrival of her
beloved husband.

Wind Walker thought of the woman who
had stolen his heart away. Even though she
was white, and even though it was taboo, he
could not help but hope Maggie would care for
him. But how could he fight off the feelings
that had claimed his heart so quickly? Destiny
had brought them together. And destiny

would pave the way for them to remain to-gether.

Chief Half Moon coughed that strange strangling cough again, bringing Wind Walker's attention back to him. He shoved aside the pelts that covered him.

Wind Walker helped his chief from beneath the pelts. He gently slid his arms beneath Half Moon, slowly lifting his frail body into them. After his chief was comfortably positioned against Wind Walker's chest, light as a feather now after losing so much weight, Wind Walker carried him from his lodge.

It was too early in the day for anyone in the village to be awake. The solitude made it harder for Wind Walker to endure the heart-wrenching task. He wondered if his chief's voice was strong enough to carry into the wind and farther still into the sky. Would the Golden Eagle Clan of Cheyenne's people be sum-moned from their lodges by the mournful sound of the song?

He glanced over at his lodge. Would she hear the song? Would it frighten her?

His chief whispered a prayer to prepare for his song as Wind Walker continued to the riverbank.

"I must have the strength to do this on my own," Half Moon said, as Wind Walker gently eased his chief from his arms. "Place me on my knees, Wind Walker. *Maheo* will lend me the strength to sing my song. It is to *Maheo* that I will be singing, as well as those in the heavens who are looking down, watching."

Wind Walker placed the chief on his knees, lifting his long gray hair so that it lay on the ground behind him. His robe made of bluish black panther skin was spread out around him.

Wind Walker wasn't sure if he should stay beside his chief in case he should fall, or leave him to this heartfelt deed that was required before he started the long road to *Se-han*.

"I will be fine," Half Moon said as he gave Wind Walker a weak smile. "Sit. Listen. You, too, will one day sing such a song."

Wind Walker returned his smile, sat down, and listened. His heart went out to the man he had loved for so long, who had taught him many things even his father had not.

It would be hard to lose him. It would be hard to have one more empty space inside his heart that a loved one always left behind.

Half Moon bowed low until his face touched the ground, then began singing his song of death. Wind Walker could not fight back his tears as they fell from his eyes.

Maggie had been awakened earlier by a bird, but now she was hearing a different song. A man was singing something so sad it touched her heart. She went to the entrance flap.

The sun was splashing its glorious colors across the sky. The sweet autumn air was tinged with the smoke that spiraled from the smoke holes of the tepees.

Maggie saw the people of the village standing just outside their lodges, tears streaming from their eyes as they gazed toward the river.

Maggie's eyes followed their same path. She saw an old man kneeling beside the river with his face touching the ground. His long gray hair was spread out upon the earth behind him as he sang a song that touched every living thing with its mournful sadness.

Someone sobbed out his name as they all reached their hands out toward him. This was Chief Half Moon.

Her eyes went quickly to Wind Walker, who sat not that far from his chief. She was touched when she saw that Wind Walker was crying. He had shown her nothing but kindness, and now it was so moving to see his respect and love for his old, ill chief.

Maggie suddenly felt safe in this village. She realized she should be thankful being here instead of at Archy's, and she was glad she had not left the village in the middle of the night where she could have been lost.

Brought back to the scene before her, Maggie

became aware that she no longer heard the old man's voice. She watched as Wind Walker gently lifted the chief into his arms and carried him back toward a large tepee.

Everything within Maggie went warm when Wind Walker looked over and found her watching him. When their eyes met and held, Maggie realized that he felt as much for her as she did for him. Unsure of how to react to such a revelation, Maggie hurriedly closed the entrance flap and went back to the warmth of the blankets and pelts. Then she waited breathlessly for him to come to his lodge, and . . . her.

Chapter 15

He doth give his joy to all:
He becomes as infant small,
He becomes a man of woe,
He doth feel the sorrow too.
    —William Blake

"Pa, wake up," Jeremy cried as he yanked on Archy's blanket and then his hand.

Archy's eyes flew open. He leaned up on an elbow and glared at his younger son. "Get out of my bedroom!" he shouted. "Leave me alone. You and your brother have been told never to enter my bedroom. Never!"

"But, Pa, the pretty lady is gone," Jeremy said, tears running from his eyes.

That got Archy's quick attention. He bolted upward and scooted to the edge of the bed. He grabbed Jeremy by the shoulders and shook him.

"Stop lying!" he shouted. "Haven't I told you that little boys who lie are eaten by bears?"

"Pa, I'm sorry," Jeremy gulped out. His eyes

grew wide and wild. "Pa, please don't let bears eat me."

Kevin was suddenly there. He gave his father an apologetic look. "I'm sorry, Pa. I didn't know Jeremy was coming here or I'd have stopped him."

"Just get him outta here," Archy ordered.

Kevin swallowed hard, nodded, then grabbed Jeremy by a hand and hurried him out of the room.

"Why'd you do that, Jeremy?" Kevin asked, his voice drawn. "Why would you go and tell Pa about the lady being gone? You should be happy that Maggie got away. She's the lucky one."

Archy had stepped out into the corridor, but stopped once he heard what his older son had said. His face drained of color because he knew that what Jeremy had said was true. Somehow Maggie had managed to escape. After all of his threats, she had still escaped!

Shouting obscenities, Archy hurried back into his bedroom. He grabbed the breeches and shirt that he had thrown to the floor the night before and yanked them on. Grumbling to himself, he pulled on his socks and boots before he grabbed a whip that he always left hanging on the wall just inside his bedroom door, the same whip he used on cowhands when they became useless and lazy.

Well, today someone was guilty of lapsing in his duty where Maggie was concerned. He had sent word among his men to decide who would stand guard at strategic places on his ranch to make certain that Maggie couldn't escape.

Archy hurried to her room first. The door was closed. He quickly opened it, slamming the door back against the wall with a loud bang.

His breath quickened as his anger grew when he saw that Maggie wasn't there. She had been in the bed, however. The bedspread was thrown back, the crumpled blankets and the imprint of her head in the feather pillow was evidence that she had slept there. But for how long?

His eyes slid to the window and he saw that it was open. She had been warned about the men guarding her. She had known that if she attempted to leave, she would be caught quickly and brought back. The cowhands posted outside were supposed to guarantee that.

It seemed that someone either forgot to keep a close eye, or someone went to sleep on the job.

He looked toward his bunkhouse. His men were sleepily emerging as they prepared to do their morning chores.

Archy was humiliated that the woman so easily slipped through his fingers. He swore he would teach the broad a thing or two, his vengeance was so strong within him. He shouted from the window at the men, cursing them. They stopped with their eyes wide in wonder.

"Just you stay put!" Archy bellowed. "Don't none of you take another step. I'm coming out there. We've a thing or two to settle, and Lord help the one who let me down last night."

Still clutching the lethal-looking whip, his face flushed red with anger, Archy hurried outside. He paced slowly before his men, looking each squarely in the eye, intimidating them even before they knew why he was so angry. They stood stiffly as Archy said nothing. His eyes narrowed angrily and he glared into one man's eyes and then another's, until he had looked into each of their eyes at least twice.

He stopped then and waved the whip in the air. "Who's going to be the recipient of this, this morning?" he shouted, his eyes filled with anger. "Who's responsible for the lady being gone? Who didn't stand their post and let her slip past?"

When no one responded, Archy was filled with venomous rage. He snapped the whip against the ground, once, then twice, each time causing the men to flinch as though he had used it on them.

"You who are guilty of sleeping on the job, speak up, or you'll all get a taste of my whip today," Archy warned.

The man who had been dropped by someone hitting him over the head refused to answer and hoped Archy wouldn't carry out his threat. Although his thick hair covered the lumps at the back of his head well enough, if Archy looked closely enough he would know who to use the whip on.

Archy didn't mind using a whip on someone when they deserved a whipping, but he was afraid of an uprising if he took the whip to them all. He knew that some of them were already disgruntled by his iron-fist rule. He wasn't sure just how far he could go before they all rode out on him, leaving him to care for his herd by himself.

No. He wasn't ready for that.

But Archy's fear extended further. What if Maggie had told her uncle about the kidnapping? He would report Archy's evildoings at the fort.

Fort Bent was set back from the route they were traveling, but they could be there in a heartbeat to report him if they knew where to look.

The cavalry would come for Archy and take

everything away from him. They could imprison him, or even hang him.

Archy knew he must stop Maggie and her uncle.

"All right," Archy said, holding the whip down at his side. "Let me explain something to all of you. If that lady tattles on me, the whole United States cavalry will come down hard on this ranch. And if I'm convicted, you all could be accused of being my accomplices. If I hang, you just might be hanging beside me."

He saw his threat jar some nerves. Uneasiness settled in their eyes. They were anxious.

"So how's it to be, men?" he shouted. "Will you ride with me today and silence that wench?"

"What do you plan to do?" one of the men braved to ask.

"Well, let me tell you, gents, what I have in mind is something more exciting than branding longhorns," Archy said, chuckling. "I need volunteers. The rest of you, get busy. There's a lot of chores to be done today."

He slid a glance over at Cookie, his fat, slovenly friend.

"I'll go on to the kitchen," Cookie grumbled. "I don't want no part in what you might have planned, otherwise."

"See to the kids, too, Cookie," Archy said as Cookie ambled heavy-legged toward the front door of the ranch house.

Cookie nodded and hurried on into the house.

The men stood back from Archy, looking at him uneasily.

"Well?" Archy spat out. "Who's riding with me today? Step forth."

Most of them stepped forward. The other few gave Archy a troubled gaze, then turned and walked in the opposite direction.

Archy smiled at those obedient to him. "It's their loss," he said, laughing flippantly. "Now gather close. Here's my plan. . . ."

When he was finished with telling them, the color had drained from their faces, but they did not back down. They went to the corral and readied their horses.

Archy rode out ahead of them. A thick cloud of dust was stirred up by the thundering of the horse's hooves across the land, the destination—the Ute stronghold, and then the wagon train.

Chapter 16

Goodbye to the Life I used to live—
And the World I used to know—
                    —Emily Dickinson

"Maggie White Woman, I have brought you something to wear," a voice said from outside Wind Walker's tepee. Maggie sprang quickly to her feet. "Wind Walker asked me to bring you one of my dresses since you and I are of the same size. I have also brought you moccasins. Can I bring them inside to you?"

Maggie was surprised by the strange name Maggie White Woman. It took her a moment to comprehend the meaning of her new name. A small smile touched her lips as she realized the woman's innocent mistake. She wondered exactly what Wind Walker had told the woman.

Then another thought occurred to her. Who was this woman to Wind Walker?

Cold fear stabbed at Maggie's heart, though

she quickly pushed the feeling away. She knew she had no claim to Wind Walker. If the woman were attached to him in some manner, it would make no difference to Maggie despite the jealousy she felt.

"Maggie White Woman?" the voice called. "Are you in there?"

Realizing that she had made the woman wait too long already, Maggie went to the entrance flap and swept it aside. "Yes, I am here," she said. Her eyes took in the beauty of the woman standing before her. She had a dress draped over her arm and held a pair of moccasins in her hand.

The woman looked no older than Maggie. Her dark eyes twinkled with mild curiosity as she smiled at her.

"I am Little Sparrow and have brought moccasins for you. And I think the dress might be more appropriate for day wear than what you are wearing," Little Sparrow said, her smile broadening as she held out the dress and moccasins to Maggie.

Maggie eagerly accepted the moccasins first and stepped into them. Her feet had felt like ice since Wind Walker had taken her from the ranch house.

"Now the dress," Little Sparrow said. "I recently finished sewing the beads on it and I have not worn it yet."

Maggie was taken by this woman's generous offer. It was obvious the amount of work that had been put into making such an elaborate dress. And here she was, giving it to a stranger.

"Thank you," Maggie said, as she took the dress. She was shocked at how heavy it was. "Thank you for your kindness, Little Sparrow."

"If you would like, I will explain to you the meaning of the designs on the dress," Little Sparrow said, looking past Maggie into the tepee.

"Yes, thank you." Maggie stepped aside so that Little Sparrow could enter. "I believe I have a while before Wind Walker returns, and then I must get ready to leave. I am to be reunited with my uncle at the wagon train. I shall return your dress and moccasins to you then."

"No, that will not be necessary," Little Sparrow said as she brushed past Maggie. "When I give a gift, it is forever."

Maggie hoped she hadn't insulted the lovely woman. She wasn't sure about the etiquette involved in gift giving with Indians. It was probably not polite to return it.

"I will be glad to keep them," Maggie said quietly.

Maggie sat down beside the fire as Little Sparrow sat on the pelts close beside her, spreading the dress out over her and Maggie's laps.

"First, I will show you the design on the back and explain its meaning to you," Little Sparrow said, pointing out the intricate design of an eagle.

"It's so pretty," Maggie remarked. "So lifelike."

"*Nai-ish*, which in Cheyenne means 'thank you.' I try to make all my designs beautiful. But when I place a depiction of an animal or bird, especially a golden eagle, it is my desire to make them as realistic as possible," Little Sparrow said, her smile bigger than before.

It was obvious to Maggie that she had just paid Little Sparrow a big compliment, and it made her feel relaxed. Maggie felt as though a bond was forming between them.

"I beaded the golden eagle on the back, not only because it is the bird of our clan, but also for it to protect me," Little Sparrow explained. She smiled at Maggie again. "I feel you may need the protection of the golden eagle. There are many bad men, red-skinned and white, alike, that would harm innocent travelers."

"I know, and you are so very kind to concern yourself about me," Maggie said, humbled by the generous nature of the Cheyenne.

"Do you see the design of eagle feathers?" Little Sparrow asked, slowly running a hand across one of them.

"Yes," Maggie answered.

"There are twenty beaded feathers to signify twenty different members of my family," Little Sparrow said. "If I would have kept the dress for myself, my family would be with me at all times."

"If it was made with such intention, are you certain you want me to have it?" she asked softly. "Perhaps there is another dress without so much meaning."

"All the dresses I make have their own significant meaning," Little Sparrow sighed. She reached a hand to her necklace. "This necklace of braided sweet grass was a gift to me from an elder. All gifts are special in their own way."

"What you have given me is very, very special, indeed," Maggie said, slowly running her hand over the golden eagle again. "I cannot thank you enough."

"Let us turn the dress over to see the front," Little Sparrow said as she turned it with Maggie's help.

"I do not use a lazy stitch, which is a whole line of beads held with a single thread," Little Sparrow said. "Instead, I stitched every other bead, using two needles, one to string the beads, and the other to anchor them to the base."

"I wish I could learn," Maggie began, but stopped when Wind Walker came into the tepee. He smiled from her to Little Sparrow.

"I see that your gifts are warmly welcomed," Wind Walker said to Little Sparrow, sitting opposite the lodge fire from the women.

"The dress is beautiful and the moccasins are welcomed relief to my feet," Maggie responded.

Little Sparrow eased the dress onto Maggie's lap and stood. She started toward the entryway, but stopped to smile first at Wind Walker and then at Maggie. "I will go now," she announced. "I enjoyed talking with you, Maggie White Woman."

Maggie glanced over at Wind Walker and saw a warm twinkle in his eyes at her new name.

Maggie smiled up at Little Sparrow. "I enjoyed meeting you. Perhaps we can talk some more before I leave."

"That would please me very much," Little Sparrow said, then hurried from the lodge.

"I see you enjoyed her company," Wind Walker said as he reached for a log and placed it in the firepit. "One day, some warrior will be lucky when he chooses her for his bride."

"You seem to care for her," Maggie said guardedly. "Is she . . . uh . . . special to you?"

"Yes, she is special to me. We are of the same clan," Wind Walker answered, resting his hands on his knees as he folded his legs before him. "I might have asked her to be my bride, but people of the same clan cannot marry. I enjoy her company. She and my wife were best friends."

"Wife?" Maggie's heart was sinking.

"My wife has been dead for three moons now," Wind Walker said. "It is not easy to talk about."

"I'm so sorry if I . . ." Maggie stopped herself when she saw the hurt it caused Wind Walker to talk about his wife.

"How is your chief faring?" she asked instead.

"He is not of this earth for much longer," Wind Walker said, frowning. "My people have one last thing to do to honor him. It is imperative that I, as the next chief, prepare and join the Massaum of Crazy Lodge Ceremony."

"You mean *after* you take me to my uncle," Maggie said guardedly. "Wind Walker, you *do* plan to take me to the wagon train this morning, don't you?"

"Please believe me when I tell you that you will be reunited with your uncle soon," Wind Walker replied. "I have your welfare in mind. But I also have my chief to see to. He takes precedence over anyone or anything else."

Maggie felt the color drain from her face. "Are you saying that I have to wait until after the ceremony before you take me to my uncle? Please don't do this. Please take me to my uncle first. He is in danger. Archy might think that I went back to the wagon train. He'll be out for blood—mine and my uncle's—and perhaps everyone else's at the wagon train."

Maggie knew that Wind Walker was about to become involved in a very important ceremony, but she was concerned about her uncle's safety. Now that her parents were gone, Red was the only family she had left.

"If you have to be involved in the ceremony, then please let another warrior take me to my uncle," she reasoned.

"All of my people's prayers and thoughts are on their ailing chief." Wind Walker shook his head. "It would not be right for me to ask any of them to leave now. I sent a scout to your uncle last night. He should be returning soon, and your uncle should be close behind. After they arrive, I will advise your uncle to report Archy, though he will have to wait until I am able to ride with him. You will need many warriors to escort you to Fort Bent. I know the colonel in charge there."

Wind Walker felt she was safer with him for now. At least until Colonel Braddock at Fort Bent sent soldiers to arrest Archy.

Maggie was relieved that Wind Walker had sent a scout to the wagon train to retrieve her uncle. But then another thought occurred to her. What if this was a ploy to keep her with him? She had no proof that anything he told her was true. Had she trusted him too easily?

Maggie pushed her doubts aside. She couldn't be wrong about him. She could only hope that he had rescued her for the right reasons.

And if she were to be truthful to herself, Maggie knew that her reluctance to believe the worst of him was due to her growing attraction. Surely her feelings for him were not misplaced. Thus far, he had given her no reason to disbelieve him.

"I have no more time to discuss this with you," Wind Walker said, rising. "My chief awaits me. Even as we talk, warriors are carrying dry branches to make a big tepee-shaped fire called a *skunk* for the ceremony."

He walked around his lodge fire and reached his hands out for Maggie. She pushed herself up from the pelts, her insides glowing warm when he gently took her hands in his.

"I would like for you to join my people at the ceremony," he said. "It will help with the passing of time as you wait for your uncle to arrive. This ceremony is very important to my chief. Soon I will have fulfilled my promise to you and your uncle. But for now, I must fulfill my promise to my chief and people."

At first Maggie hesitated. But she was intrigued. The ceremony sounded mystical.

"Yes, I will join you," she said. "I am touched that you would want me to."

"I will leave you to change into the dress; then I will come for you," Wind Walker said, his voice pleased, his eyes warm.

Maggie gazed into their dark depths, hypnotized by the gentleness she saw within them. Wind Walker slid his arms around her waist.

"I wish to kiss you," he said huskily.

All warnings of whether or not she should trust him were forgotten. Maggie could not deny herself this one chance.

She slowly twined her arms around his neck, and his lips joined hers in a wondrously soft kiss. His strong body leaned into hers, blotting any doubt that she ever had of him.

Suddenly she knew without a doubt that she had found the man she had been put on this earth for. She was in love. And she would not allow herself to think of the word *forbidden*.

Chapter 17

Secure against its own,
No treason it can fear;
Itself its sovereign, of itself
The soul should stand in awe.
          —Emily Dickinson

Archy loped to the top of a ridge and looked down at the wagon train. His men and several Indians waited for him, including Dark Arrow, the Ute renegade everyone feared.

In the past, Archy had joined with Dark Arrow often, both gaining wealth as they came together against whites.

Today Dark Arrow and his Ute renegades had made a pact with Archy and his cowhands. In exchange for Dark Arrow's support, the renegades could have the loot they stole from the wagon train, but Archy got the woman.

Archy knew that most of his cowhands felt more at ease going against a wagon train of whites if the Utes were there to assist them. The renegades under Dark Arrow's lead were known for their cunning and shrewdness. If they were with Dark Arrow, they would have a better chance of riding away from today's ambush alive.

Archy edged his horse over close to Dark Arrow's. "You know the plan. Me and my men'll ride toward the wagon train. When we get halfway there, come out of hiding and attack with us. But remember, Dark Arrow, your men are not to harm the redheaded woman. I want her alive. I've a thing or two to teach that wench."

Dark Arrow nodded, smiling crookedly. "You go ahead. We follow. The woman is yours, but all that is in the wagons belongs to us Ute!"

"Yeah, sure," Archy assented, nodding. He looked over his shoulder at his men. "It's time. If any of you are having second thoughts, you'd best speak up now. No harm'll come to you for backing out."

He smiled maliciously at the men. They knew that if any of them backed out of the planned ambush now, they'd pay with their hides. No one ever got a second chance with Archy.

"Well, looks as though you still want to be a part of this, so let's go," Archy said, resting his hand on his holstered pistol at his right side.

"Remember, don't get antsy. We've got to look peaceful-like in order to get close enough to the wagon train."

Archy knew that if Maggie were there, she would have warned the others about him. The fight would begin the moment Archy and his men were spied riding toward them.

"If they start shooting at us earlier than expected, shoot back and don't spare the ammunition," Archy ordered. "There's more where that came from."

Archy gave Dark Arrow a mock salute, then flicked his reins against the horse's flesh and thundered down the hillside. His only objective was to get Maggie. She would pay for making him look like a fool.

Hooves churned upon the earth, drumming the molten morning. Dust rose up in a golden fountain of spray as Archy rode along the straight stretch of ground. His eyes narrowed angrily on the wagon train. They had to have seen him and his men approaching by now.

If Maggie saw him at the lead, surely she would know why he was coming and bringing so many of his cowhands.

"Wait'll she sees the renegades," Archy said through gritted teeth as he pushed his horse faster toward the wagon train.

* * *

Red heard the sound of horses approaching in the distance. He grabbed his rifle and ran between two wagons.

His throat went dry when he saw just how many men were approaching,

"What's going on?" Clarence Klein asked as he ran up beside Red. "Lord a'mighty, look at the amount of men. Thank the Lord they're white-skinned."

"If one of those men is Archibald Parrish, then I'd say we did the right thing by sending all of the children and as many women as could get into two wagons ahead to find a fort," Red said, his hand tightly clutching his rifle. "I felt like a sitting duck after Wind Walker's scout came and told us where they had found Maggie. Now, it looks like I may never see her again, after all."

"What are you saying?" Clarence asked.

Red's heart had sunk the moment he recognized Archy. "Do you see the man who seems to be leading the others? He and I have a score to settle today."

Red knew that he had been right to send ahead as many as he could. The men, and the few women who wouldn't leave their husbands' sides, stayed behind with Red until Maggie was returned.

Now Red wished that he had ordered everyone ahead. But the men who'd been his friends since childhood just wouldn't abandon him and Maggie. Now it looked as though their loyalty might result in their deaths.

Red looked anxiously around him. He hoped there were enough wagons left in the circle for Archy not to realize that some had left.

If they could get a volley of bullets firing before Archy got to the wagons, it might encourage the cowards to turn back. Red was gambling with time. He knew that the scout hadn't had the chance to return to the Cheyenne village yet.

"Spread the word!" Red shouted. "Everyone! Grab your guns! Get ready to fire as soon as those men get close enough!"

There was a scurry of feet as men came with their rifles and pistols to make a straight line of fire in front of the wagons.

"What if they're coming in peace?" Mick Womack asked, keeping his firearm steady and aiming at the approaching men.

"Look past them and see who else is approaching now, and then I think you'll have your answer," Red said as renegades poured down the hillside, joining Archy and his men.

Loud war cries split the air as the horses thundered onward. Rifles were carried by both red- and white-skinned men, though most of the renegades opted for their bows and arrows.

"Now!" Red cried. "Start firing. Get off as many rounds as you can. Pray, too, for I don't think we have a chance in hell of surviving this ambush. Damn that Archy. Damn him to hell!"

Red began firing, and as he did, his life passed before his eyes. He remembered Maggie's sweet smile and could hear her gentle laughter. He comforted himself with the knowledge that at least she was safe from dying at the hands of madmen whites and red-skinned renegades.

"Run for cover!" Red shouted, knowing that it was foolish to stand out in the open. It was evident that there were too many of them.

Red scrambled with the other men behind the wagons. The remaining women ran to their husbands, crying and clutching at them, just as the roar of horse's hooves went past the wagons, the hiss of arrows and the popping of bullets announcing their arrival.

Archy rode past, firing aimlessly, then wheeled his horse quickly around and started riding toward Red again. Red turned and tried to run away when he felt a sting of fire in his back and was thrown face forward onto the ground. "Maggie," he whispered, his fingers slowly releasing their hold on his rifle. "My sweet Maggie . . ."

"Damn it all to hell. I didn't want the women killed!" Archy screamed, his face flushed. "I thought I made it clear that I want Maggie alive!"

Dark Arrow moved to his side on his black steed. "No one tells Dark Arrow what to do. When I ambush, I kill. If women get in the way, they are downed with the men." He shrugged idly. "The women got in the way. They are now dead."

Archy knew there was a threat behind the renegade's words. "You were hell-bent on killing everyone even though you knew my main purpose was to get a woman, to get Maggie!" he said between clenched teeth.

Dark Arrow laughed as he rode away from Archy. He shouted to the renegades to take what they could from the wagons and put it into one wagon to transport to their hideout.

Archy looked slowly around at the fallen. Maggie's uncle lay on his belly, his blood spread out like ink on a blotter all along the back of his shirt. The kind of wound that was caused by one of Archy's bullets. Archy had fired recklessly into the crowd. And although he had aimed at Red, he had thought that he had missed him.

But here was the proof that he hadn't.

Archy had killed today. Other times when he had rode with Dark Arrow, they had not killed so many. They had left the travelers tied to the wheels of their wagons, merciful enough to let them live. But today? He could not help but shudder as he saw the arrows lodged into the backs of so many innocent people.

At least when this massacre was discovered, the Utes would be blamed. Archy didn't care. Although he had tried to protect them before, this time he would be glad when they were caught. The damn Utes had not done anything he'd said. They had ignored him!

As long as no one was alive to point an accusing finger at him, Archy was safe.

"But what of Maggie?" he asked himself, now riding around the dead, his eyes searching. He looked at the hair color of the few women there. None was as brilliantly red as Maggie's had been.

"Damn it all to hell," he cursed. "All of this for nothing! She isn't even here."

He wheeled his horse around to ride from the wagon train. Ignoring the Utes who were throwing things from the wagons, Archy looked over his shoulder at his men. They were as pale as ghosts. None of them had ever been a part of anything like this before.

Some were puking. A few were crying.

"Come on!" he cried. "Let's get outta here!"

Yes, it was time to get away from the massacre. He would save his own hide. He must return to his ranch and look as though nothing had happened.

He glowered at his men as they hurried on their horses behind him. "If any of you are ever questioned about this, you'd better stay quiet," he shouted. "You see how easily people die? You could die as quickly. *I'd* kill you."

When he saw that he had sent fear straight into their hearts, Archy sank his heels into the flanks of his horse and rode hard in the direction of his ranch.

He looked over his shoulder at the wagon train. All the wagons were aflame except for the one that would carry the loot back to the Ute hideout. He counted the wagons.

Something didn't seem right. Archy thought back to the first time he entered the camp. Hadn't there been more women? And hell, where were the children?

He went cold inside. He knew he had been duped. Surely the other wagons had been sent on. They could have reached Fort Bent by now.

If Maggie was with those who had escaped,

she would have enough to tell to get him hanged.

The thought made him ill, but he had no choice other than to wait it out.

Perhaps he was wrong. Just perhaps Maggie had not found her way back to the wagon train after all.

Archy dismissed his worries. He was still as safe as anyone else in this crazy, untamed land!

Chapter 18

I only hear above his place of rest
Their tender undertone,
The infinite longings of a troubled breast,
The voice so like his own.
          —Henry Wadsworth Longfellow

Maggie was wearing the lovely Indian dress
that Little Sparrow had given to her. Her hair
was woven into two long braids that hung
down her back.

She had loved to wear braids when she was
a child. Maggie would never forget how lovingly her mother had braided her hair, tying
satin ribbons on each.

Maggie had so many fond memories of her
mother to enjoy. She was glad to be able to set
aside her sadness and guilt. Strange as it
seemed, Wind Walker had not only freed her of
her captivity at Archy's ranch, but also her in-
ability to be happy again since her mother's
death.

Until now, she couldn't remember things of

the past or her mother without it tearing at her heart. Now her memories gave her pangs of sweetness.

She wasn't sure how it could happen, but being with Wind Walker had lifted burdens from her heart.

Maggie felt beautiful as she walked at Wind Walker's side toward the crowd that sat in a wide semicircle in the center of the village where the ceremony was going to be held. The large tepee-shaped fire called a *skunk* burned at the center of the crowd of Cheyenne.

As they approached the people, Maggie became aware of the looks she was receiving.

Some of the women stared at her with resentment, while other women gave her encouraging smiles.

Maggie returned the smiles, glad that some of them did not think of her as an interference in their lives.

She then noticed the men. They seemed to be looking at her with keen interest. Maggie quickly forced her focus on what everyone wore today.

The women were lovely in their colorful, fringed buckskin garments, decorated with beads and porcupine quills. The warriors were dressed in fancy attire. Wind Walker looked very handsome in his buckskins, which were fringed and beaded. The young girls' faces were glowing like bright red autumn leaves, their glossy braids falling over each ear.

Maggie saw Little Sparrow walking toward her and Wind Walker, smiling and holding her hands out for Maggie. She wore a necklace of blue beads, and her heavy black hair lay across her shoulders, braidless, then down to her waist.

"Maggie White Woman, come and sit with me," Little Sparrow said, taking one of Maggie's hands. She grinned at Wind Walker. "I shall make her comfortable while you do your duty to our chief."

Wind Walker affectionately brushed a kiss across Little Sparrow's cheek. "Your heart is big. *Nai-ish*, thank you."

He gave Maggie a soft smile, then hurried away.

Little Sparrow giggled. "He is the big brother I never had. I love him like a brother."

Maggie was relieved. She hated to think that both Little Sparrow and Wind Walker regretted being of the same clan, which forbade them from loving each other. They were good friends, and the part of Maggie's heart that had felt jealousy over Wind Walker's behavior toward Little Sparrow could relax.

She reminded herself that she should not care one way or another how Wind Walker *or* Little Sparrow felt toward each other.

Soon she would be gone. She would be re-united with her uncle, and their journey to Oregon would be resumed.

But she knew that when she thought of Wind Walker, she would remember her feelings for him. That if she were free to, she would have loved him as a woman loves a man she has given her life to.

"I have made a place for us here," Little Sparrow said, nodding toward a pallet of blankets and pelts that had been placed between two other women.

As Maggie sat down, she could feel the heat of the large fire on her cheeks, even though it was quite far from her. Her eyes went past the fire, and she saw at one end a space had been left in the semicircle, where a large tepee had been erected. It was much larger than Wind Walker's, and even the chief's. It looked like it could hold many people within it.

Everyone from the village had come from their lodges to participate in the ceremony. The children were sitting quietly with their parents, their eyes anxious one moment, somber the next, as they looked toward their chief's tepee, which sat just back from the crowd, opposite to where the larger tepee had been placed for the ceremony.

She had seen Wind Walker go inside the chief's lodge, and waited and watched along with everyone else for their chief to be brought from his home.

A plush pile of pelts and blankets had been prepared for him with room left on each side. She wondered if the old chief would be strong enough to sit, or if he would need to lay down during the ceremony. Maggie didn't know much about his condition except for what Wind Walker had told her. But she saw sadness in many of the women's eyes and assumed it was because they were worried about their chief.

Maggie's eyes were drawn quickly back to the chief's lodge when Wind Walker suddenly appeared with the old chief held lovingly in his arms. She could not help but love him, even if she had to love him silently. Maggie felt a warmth circle her heart as she watched him bring the old man out, then place him on his thick pad of pelts and blankets. The elderly chief stretched out on his back, seemingly unable to sit.

The chief wore a beautiful robe of panther skins, bluish black in color as the sun fell upon it. His gray hair fell down his back in two long braids and he wore one lone feather affixed in a loop of his hair.

Maggie saw how gaunt the chief was. His eyes were sunken and his mouth was strangely twisted as he attempted to smile at the children as they came and took turns kneeling beside him, hugging him.

Wind Walker said something to the children, which caused them to return to their blankets beside their mothers.

She looked around and saw the utter devotion to Wind Walker in his people's eyes. Wind Walker seemed to be everything to them. Maggie could see how so easily he could become everything to a woman.

She wished she could be that woman, then blushed at the thought.

Her eyes were drawn again to the huge tepee set up just behind the half circle of people, its doorway facing east. Warriors dressed as buffalo began leaving the tepee in single file. They each carried buffalo heads made of grass with horns on them.

They went and stood before their chief. The leader raised a cloth in the air and held it there as one of the other warriors pretended to give the chief medicine. The one holding the cloth brought it down and around the chief several times, then those dressed as buffalo went back inside the huge tepee.

More warriors came from the same tepee, but they were dressed like deer. They wore caps with leather on them cut out like deer horns. They charged each other from different directions, until they had done this ritual four times, stopping when they reached their chief.

Then they, too, returned to the large tepee.

Maggie's eyes widened when more warriors came from the tepee, this time painted colorfully as clowns. They came slowly up to their chief, then ran back from him, pretending to be afraid, then went back again, walking on their toes, as softly as they could.

Suddenly, they jumped high in the air over their chief without touching him.

They then returned to the large tepee, also.

Soon all the performers came from the tepee and began to dance as distant drums played steady beats, as others kept time with rattles. The dance was vigorous, almost frenzied.

The men dressed as buffalo started dancing around the fire, stamping the ground and snorting, hitting the ground with one foot, then the other, shuffling their feet slowly, then to the left.

Suddenly they stopped and those dressed as deer ran from the circle of people and went to the river. The crowd stood and stepped back far enough for their chief to see those warriors at the river.

Maggie stood beside Little Sparrow, glancing over at Wind Walker as he still sat with his chief.

She turned her attention again to the warriors dressed as deer. They were now in the water.

The clowns followed them into the water, and then the buffalo pretended to chase the deer and clowns.

The clowns pretended to shoot arrows at the deer.

One of the buffalo revealed his power as he blew something that looked like a cotton fluff four or five feet into the air. It scattered and disappeared.

A woman dancer suddenly appeared at the water's edge, who soon pretended to be shot, and fell to the ground, silent. The dancers in the water stopped and grew quiet as they stared at the fallen maiden.

Then the woman rose from the ground, smiling, and the warriors in the water came to shore, also smiling. They went to their chief and took turns embracing him, signaling that the ceremony was over.

Maggie watched Wind Walker carry his chief back inside the chief's lodge as the crowd dispersed, leaving Maggie and Little Sparrow.

"Wind Walker asked me to ask you to wait here for him," Little Sparrow said. She gave Maggie a hug, then left for her own lodge.

Maggie felt suddenly ill at ease standing alone where the ceremony had been held. The fire still burned high, popping and crackling not that far from where she stood.

She felt alone, misplaced . . . and dispirited.

Chapter 19

Love conquers all things;
Let us, too, surrender to love.
—Virgil

It seemed as if she had stood alone forever, though it had been only moments, before Wind Walker came from the lodge and joined her.

"Chief Half Moon is now resting comfortably," he said, smiling at Maggie as they walked toward his tepee together. "Our shaman sits with him now."

"How is he otherwise? Did the ceremony help him?" Maggie asked. "It was quite fascinating to watch."

"The ceremony has given my chief a peaceful heart, as it did for our people," Wind Walker said. "Now *Maheo* decides the rest."

"Maheo?" Maggie asked, forking an eyebrow. "What—or should I say who—is Maheo?"

Wind Walker stepped to his tepee and held the entrance flap aside for Maggie so that she could enter his lodge before him. "*Maheo* is everything to us Cheyenne," he said, following her inside. "You pray to your God. We pray to our *Maheo*."

"Lately, I have whispered many prayers to my God that my uncle and everyone at the wagon train is safe," Maggie said, turning to Wind Walker as he stepped up to her. "Wind Walker, *now* can you take me to the wagon train? You have done your duty to your chief. Can you now please help me? I want to see if my uncle is all right."

"You do not need to go to him. He is coming to you," Wind Walker said. He took her hands and gazed into her eyes. "As I said, I sent my scout Black Hawk to tell your uncle that you are here and that you are safe."

He didn't tell her that Black Hawk had not returned yet. Wind Walker did not know if he had given Red the message. He expected his scout to arrive ahead of Red. But now he was afraid that something might have happened to both Black Hawk and Red. He didn't think it wise to tell Maggie, though. He did not want to worry her needlessly.

Wind Walker had learned long ago not to speculate so much over things. Since the arrival of the white man to his land, he had learned that things did not always go as he would expect.

For now, he would just hope for the best. Especially since he was alone again with Maggie, and he had done all that he could for his chief.

As he and Maggie gazed into each other's eyes, silence spread between them. Wind Walker was being swallowed whole by his feelings for her.

He could tell that she was enjoying this time alone as much as he. It was in her eyes. It was in her rapid heartbeat, which was noticeable in the vein of her throat.

Everything within him cried out to hold her again . . . to kiss her.

The way Wind Walker was looking at her, as though he knew her hidden feelings for him, Maggie suddenly felt flush inside. She had never felt so alive before. He alone was able to warm her heart and cloud her mind.

But she had to keep reminding herself that this was not any ordinary man. He was an Indian. A man whom maybe she shouldn't trust. At least until she was handed over to her uncle. Even then, she knew it wouldn't be right for either her or Wind Walker to let their feelings for each other show.

She was white.

He was red.

And she . . .

Suddenly Wind Walker yanked Maggie into his arms and brought his lips down hard upon hers in a kiss so hot it melted her insides.

She freely yielded to his embrace once again, and found herself returning the kiss passionately.

She was experiencing a sweet headiness.

Suddenly this man's color didn't matter, nor that he was forbidden fruit. She might be wrong to trust him, but he was the only man who stirred desire within her.

She clung and strained against him, feverish in her sudden need of a man.

There was no doubt in her heart now that although she had known him for such a short time, she had fallen, heart and soul, in love with Wind Walker.

Yet she knew that she must fight these urges.

And what if this was a part of his plan . . . to get her body aching for his, so that she might not want to join the wagon train again? How *could* she love a man she only recently met, and not just any man, an Indian!

The hungry ache between her thighs made her realize just how far the kiss and embrace had taken her, and she breathlessly yanked herself free.

Breathing hard, her face hot with a blush, Maggie stared into Wind Walker's eyes and saw hunger in their depths. She knew that there was danger in that.

"Please forget what just happened," Maggie pleaded. "Please take me to Red. I'm . . . I'm . . . tired of waiting for him. Maybe something has happened."

Wind Walker found it hard to think clearly. Every fiber of his being wanted this woman. Her straining against his body had fueled his fires.

A warrior shouted from outside his tepee, bringing him back to reality. He recognized the voice of the scout Black Hawk, whom he had sent to the wagon train.

Black Hawk shouted Wind Walker's name again in alarm. Black Hawk's horse whinnied as he brought it to a quick halt outside Wind Walker's lodge.

Maggie's heart skipped a beat when she heard the panic in the warrior's voice and could only assume that it was the scout that Wind Walker had sent to the wagon train. The blood drained from her face as she brushed past Wind Walker.

She hurried outside and looked up at the sweaty warrior. His hair had fallen partially from their braids.

"Tell me!" she cried as she gazed up into his dark, troubled eyes. "How is my uncle? Where is he?"

Wind Walker rushed to her side.

He protectively slid an arm around her waist. He was afraid that in a matter of moments she might hear news that would devastate her.

It was in Black Hawk's eyes. It was in his voice that the news was bad.

"Something has happened," Black Hawk rushed out, sliding down from his saddle.

He handed his reins to a young brave, who took the sweating, hard-breathing horse quickly away.

"I gave the man your message," Black Hawk said thickly. "I offered to wait so that he could ride with me, but he said he had some things to do first, to go ahead. I left and had gone some distance when I heard gunfire and war cries behind me. I was on a ridge. When I looked down from it, I saw the attack on the wagon train." His eyes slid over to Maggie. "I do not know how many survived, if any."

Maggie grabbed on to Wind Walker's arm. She fought off the terrible feeling of fainting. She could hardly believe what she had just heard, yet it was true.

Suddenly, she felt so ashamed. While she had been with Wind Walker, her uncle might have died.

She started running toward the corralled horses.

"I should have gone there," she cried. "I should have been with my uncle." She turned and stopped, her hands in fists at her sides. "You should have taken me! Now . . . now . . . it's too late."

Wind Walker hurried to her and grabbed her by the shoulders. He gazed into her tear-filled eyes.

"It is no one's fault but those who are wreaking havoc along the countryside. Only they are guilty. You are not. I am not. Had you been there, you would have also been a victim."

"They are probably all dead," Maggie sobbed, her heart tearing to shreds. Suddenly she flung herself into Wind Walker's arms. She looked up at him through wet eyelashes. "What am I to do? My uncle! Wind Walker, I loved him so much!"

He held her and comforted her, relieved that she wasn't casting all of the blame on him.

He turned his gaze over to Black Hawk as he held Maggie close to him, her tears wetting his buckskin shirt. "You saw who did it," he said. "Who?"

"It was the Ute renegades, and . . . the man who has taken our land and brought those long-horned animals here," he said.

Maggie's heart skipped a beat when she heard this. Then suddenly she felt her sorrow replaced by another emotion.

She *hated* that ruthless cattle baron with all of her being.

How could any man side with murdering renegades? But she had to remind herself that he was not truly a man.

He was a demon!

She yanked herself away from Wind Walker. "Take me to my uncle," she said, her voice now tight and controlled. "I want to go to my uncle."

"It would be safer for you to stay at my village while I go and check on things," Wind Walker said, taking her hands and holding them.

"But don't you see?" Maggie said, searching his eyes. "I *can't* stay here. I must go and be with my uncle. I must see for myself. And if he is dead, he needs a proper burial."

Wind Walker saw the importance of her going with him. He understood the sort of love that she had for her uncle.

He placed a finger beneath her chin and raised it until their eyes met.

"I do understand, but *you* must understand that we might come face-to-face with those who are responsible for this," he warned.

"No matter what, I will go with you," Maggie said firmly. "I must."

Somewhere in the distance, beyond the village, a young man blew his plaintive eagle wing flute, so sweet and lilting, such a contrast to how things were in Maggie's life.

"And so then you shall accompany me there," Wind Walker said.

Maggie slipped back into his arms and gave him another hug. But Wind Walker knew that she did not hug him because she was grateful, but because she felt something for him.

Just as he felt something for her.

Maggie was riding beside Wind Walker, with his warriors riding beside and behind them. She glanced over at him.

She had been wrong to doubt him. The moment he had been told about what had happened at the wagon train, she had seen the horror in his eyes. She knew that he was the sort of man she had hoped he was. He had been telling her the truth. All along, he had had her best interest at heart.

The face of her uncle came into her mind's eye, bringing fresh tears to her eyes.

First her father, then her mother, and now . . . her uncle. No. It just couldn't have happened. Without Red, she was alone in the world.

Her eyes slid over to Wind Walker. No, she wouldn't be alone.

She had Wind Walker.

Chapter 20

There in seclusion and remote from men
The wizard hand lies cold,
Which at its topmost speed let fall the pen,
And left the tale half told.
         —Henry Wadsworth Longfellow

Kevin and Jeremy's noses were pressed against the pane of their bedroom window as they watched their father arriving with his cowhands.

"I don't see her with them," Jeremy whined. "He didn't find her. I wanted Pa to find Maggie."

"You should be glad he didn't," Kevin said, though his heart had dropped when he noticed that the kind woman wasn't with his father. "At least she isn't a prisoner any longer. She's free. She's out there somewhere, free."

"But if Pa would've brought her back, I know she'd have found a way to escape again, and this time take us," Jeremy said, walking from the window. Tears spilling from his eyes, he plopped down on the edge of his bed. "Now we'll never be able to leave this place. Never!"

"When we get older I'll take you far, far away from here," Kevin reassured him as he sat down beside Jeremy. He drew his tiny-boned brother into his arms. "I promise, Jeremy. I cross my heart and hope to die."

"Mommy always said that when she made a promise," Jeremy said, turning to cling to his brother. "But it still never happened. So, Kevin, quit saying that to me, because you know we'll never be able to leave this place. Pa won't allow it. He has a lot in mind for the both of us. He'll put us to work with his cowhands. We'll just be someone else for him to order around."

Kevin held his brother safely within his arms—at least for now, while he was allowed to.

But every day brought another kind of fear into their hearts. Their father was a madman.

Kevin was as disappointed as his brother that Maggie didn't return. She had been the only ray of hope they had seen since the death of their mother. But at least Maggie was free of his father's demonic mind. He only hoped that she was safe.

Kevin jerked away from his brother with a start when the bedroom door opened with a loud bang as it slammed hard against the wall. Both children cowered. Their hearts thumped wildly within their chests as they watched their father come and stand over them, his fists on his hips, his pale blue eyes filled with a fiery rage.

"Did either of you see anyone last night?" Archy asked, his jaw tight. "Did you see Maggie leave? Did someone take her?"

He leaned down into Kevin's face. "And you'd best not lie, or you'll feel the sting of my razor strop on your backs, the both of you. Do you hear?"

"Pa, neither Jeremy or me saw anything last night," Kevin said, his voice tiny and quivering with fear. "We wuz asleep."

"We're telling the truth, Pa," Jeremy hurried out, reaching over to take Kevin's hand. "Can we go out and play now? Can we? And can we go and see the baby longhorns before they're branded? I don't like to see the brands on them. Can we go and see them now, huh, please?"

Archy stood back up, his back straight. "Yeah, go on," he said.

He watched them scurry from the room in obvious desperation to get away from him. He went to the window and watched his sons leave the house and run across the yard toward the longhorns.

For many reasons he was disappointed in them. But in one respect, he was proud. They showed a keen interest in the longhorns at their young age. They'd be valuable to him in the future when he needed extra hands.

He expected them to grow up and be as strong as their father, but he doubted they'd ever be as shrewd. Their mother had instilled too much sissiness for them ever to amount to much.

He sighed as he looked farther into the distance, where he could see smoke rising into the sky. He had left before the renegades finished their business at the wagon train. Surely the smoke was coming from the charred remains of the camp.

A chill rode his spine as he recalled the death he had left behind. He had not realized the attack would be that savage. Though he knew that it was important not to leave anyone alive who'd be able to point a finger at him or his men. At least for now, he was safe at home and had nothing that could prove his part in the raid.

He turned and walked from the children's room, and went to his study. He sat down in a plush leather armchair before the cold ashes of his fireplace.

His mind went over everything that had happened since he had stupidly stolen Maggie from the wagon train. From that point on, he had been walking a tightrope. And the only way he could get off was to find her and silence her once and for all.

"But where in the hell is she?" Archy asked, impatiently running his fingers through his long greasy hair.

He went to his liquor cabinet and poured himself a shot of whiskey, downing it in one fast, deep gulp. His anger was growing by the minute. He pitched the glass across the room, where it hit and shattered against the stone of the fireplace, landing on the hearth in tiny, twinkling pieces.

He went over everything he had done. He had checked the horses in his corral. None were missing. That meant that she had not stolen one to get away. Either someone had come for her, or she had left on foot.

"She might even be lying dead somewhere," he whispered to himself. Or someone had found her.

He recalled that not all the wagons had been in the circle during the attack. Maggie might have been rescued, then taken away on one of the wagons, which were now more than likely safely at Fort Bent. Maggie might even now be spilling her guts.

If so, the cavalry could ride up at any minute.

Then something else came to him. The Indians were cunning enough for a warrior to come

in the night and render his sentries unconscious.

"Wind Walker?" he said, his eyebrow forking.

He had seen Wind Walker arriving at the
wagon train with his pal Blue Wing. Could it
have been Wind Walker who came like a thief
in the night and taken Maggie away right from
beneath Archy's nose?

His mind was spinning with all of the possi-
bilities, but one thing was certain, he had to lay
low for some time now, in order not to get himself in trouble.

To cool off his ire, he went out and checked
on the longhorns that were fenced in closer to
the house. He looked up and saw smoke rising
in the distance, knowing its origin.

He thought about Maggie again. If she was
alive, she'd have more on her mind than him.
The massacre was way worse than a mere
abduction.

"I'll play it cool and go about my daily business as though nothing happened," he whispered to himself.

Chapter 21

But the rowen mixed with weeds,
Tangled tufts from marsh and meads,
Where the poppy drops its seeds,
    In the silence and the gloom.
        —Henry Wadsworth Longfellow

Maggie rode with Wind Walker in the direction of the black smoke in the sky. She was hardly aware of the prairie dogs. They sat erect on the edge of slightly terraced mounds that surrounded their burrows, uttering sharp, squeaky barking sounds, vigorously jerking their short tails against their backs.

All she could think about was her uncle and their fellow travelers on the wagon train, and how she might find them.

If the wagons had been set afire, surely the owners were . . .

"Be careful of the prairie dog mounds," Wind Walker warned, as he slowed his horse in order to navigate around the holes. "This prairie village is a considerable size. There are holes every few feet. Do not let your horse's hooves get caught in one."

Maggie became alert to what he had said, only now aware of the danger that lay all around her. She slowed her horse's pace and watched carefully as she led it around one hole and then another.

Finally, the dog town came to an end and the way was clear of any obstacles. They rode across a straight stretch of land, then followed Wind Walker's lead up a slope of land that led to a bluff.

Her insides tightened. She assumed this was the same bluff upon which she had seen Wind Walker the first time when he and Blue Wing came to observe the wagon train before warning them about what had now come to pass.

That day, she had been looking on the face of her destiny, for she loved Wind Walker now with every fiber of her being.

When she was in his arms, she felt such joy and peace. She felt totally loved and protected.

But her thoughts were jerked back from loving arms and sweet kisses as she got to the top of the bluff. Her heart sank when all she saw for many miles around in all directions was the black smoke from the charred remains of the wagon train. Through the thick cloud she was able to discern bodies sprawled out on the ground.

She saw no signs of life anywhere.

"Uncle Patrick," she cried. "Oh, Red, not you too!"

Wind Walker saw the destruction below them and turned quick eyes to Maggie.

"How could this be happening?" she sobbed. "Why?"

"No one knows what their fate will be until it happens," Wind Walker said, then reached a hand to her cheek. "Do you want to stay here with some of my warriors as I check for survivors?"

"No," Maggie said, wiping at the tears that flowed down her cheeks. "Although this is breaking my heart, I must go with you. If Red is among them, I want to see if he . . . if . . . he might possibly be alive. If not, then I want to give him . . . a . . . Christian burial and say words over his grave."

"You are a very courageous woman," Wind Walker said softly.

"No, not courageous," she murmured. "Devastated, sad, and . . ."

She couldn't say anything else. Tears continued to rush from her eyes. She looked away from Wind Walker and hung her head.

"Cry until there are no more tears. Then we will go onward," Wind Walker said.

His heart ached for her. He knew the sorrow of the kind of loss she was now experiencing.

He had lost many, many loved ones. He hated to see this woman whom he loved with all of his heart going through such misery. But there was nothing he could say or do now, to ease her pain. It was something that she would need to work within herself.

And if her uncle was dead, then she was alone in the world without kin.

Wind Walker wanted to be the one to lead her into her future. He wanted her in his life forever. He knew that a future without her was not a future at all.

"I'm ready," Maggie said. She wiped the last tears from her eyes. "I pray that my uncle is still alive. I pray that someone down there is alive."

"*Maheo* is with you, as is your God," Wind Walker said. He looked over his shoulder at his warriors and nodded. "It is time to proceed with our journey. But be wary. The guilty ones might be lurking close by in hopes of having someone new to ambush."

They nodded in return.

They all rode silently down the hillside and across a plot of land where autumn wildflowers were abloom and sending off their tangy smell. But the fragrance was soon mingled with the stench of the burned wagons.

Maggie blinked and rubbed at her eyes as she rode through the smoke that temporarily blinded her.

Suddenly they were there.

Maggie's despair deepened when she saw the familiar faces. So many of them were childhood friends of both her and her uncle. Due to their closeness in age, Maggie and Red had been raised as siblings.

"Red," she gulped out as she dismounted and stumbled across the ground. Scattered around her were the bodies of her friends who had been downed mostly by arrows. Her eyes searched frantically for her uncle.

Then she found him.

A deep sorrow swept through her, and she wanted to scream when she saw him lying on his belly, the back of his shirt soaked with blood. She knelt down and inspected him, quickly noticing that he had not been downed by an arrow. Yet she didn't see a bullet hole anywhere on his shirt.

"It seems the bullet only grazed him," Wind Walker said as he stepped up beside her. He knelt beside Red as Maggie moved closer to him.

"Then perhaps he wasn't mortally wounded," Maggie said. An ounce of hope rose within her. Her hand trembled as she reached for her uncle's face.

When she touched Red's cheek, her eyes widened. She looked quickly over at Wind Walker.

"His face is warm!" she cried.

She watched Wind Walker place a hand at her uncle's mouth, then smiled over at her. "He is breathing. His breath is warm," he said, now slowly turning Red over. "He is alive."

Maggie's heart started to beat again as a joy swam through her. She knelt over Red, her hand softly on his cheek.

His eyelids fluttered then slowly opened.

"Red!" she cried. "Uncle Patrick! You are alive!"

Red sputtered and choked as he tried to speak, then closed his eyes and again went unconscious.

"Wind Walker!" Maggie cried.

Wind Walker placed his hand to Red's lips again. "He is alive, but in much need of medication. Although the bullet might have only grazed his flesh, he has lost much blood."

"But surely there are no doctors anywhere near here," Maggie said anxiously. "By the time we reach a fort, my uncle might not be strong enough to make it."

"There is the shaman," Wind Walker said, drawing Maggie's attention back to him. "We will take your uncle to my village. My shaman, Sky Dreamer, will tend to your uncle's wound. Sky Dreamer is smart in all ways of medicine. He will make your uncle well and strong again."

"Yes, oh, yes, let's go now, Wind Walker," Maggie said. She rushed to her feet. "Please, let's go now."

Then she stopped and looked slowly around her and at the warriors who were going from person to person. They found no more survivors.

Maggie's heart went out to them all. She would never forget the fun and camaraderie they had somehow managed to find on this long, sad journey to Oregon. Now all that had been stolen away by mindless, heartless murderers.

She turned to Wind Walker. "How could Archy join the renegades and do something as horrible as this?"

"Because partners in crime are evil through and through," Wind Walker said, in his mind's eye seeing the face of Archibald Parrish. The man was filled with the sorts of demons that would guide him into doing such evil actions. Wind Walker had thought for some time that Archy was in alliance with the Ute renegades. How else could he live on land that once was solely the red man's without their harassment?

"How could a white man do this to other white men?" Maggie asked in bewilderment.

"Let us not talk about that now," Wind Walker encouraged. "We must get your uncle to my shaman."

Maggie shivered as she turned and looked at her fallen friends again. "They need to be buried."

"Several warriors will stay behind and see to their burial," Wind Walker said, already bending low to gently lift Red into his arms.

"I should stay, as well, and say words over their graves," Maggie said, her voice catching.

"We must get your uncle to my village quickly," Wind Walker reasoned. "Your friends would understand. They would want your uncle's interest to come first."

"Let me at least take enough time to say good-bye," Maggie replied, already stepping away from him.

After she went and said her final words to each, she went back to Wind Walker. She was amazed at what she found. Wind Walker and several others had put together a quick travois on which to carry her uncle back to the village. It was made of wood from a wagon that had not been totally burned and some canvas that had survived the fire's angry clutches.

She gave Wind Walker a smile of thank-you, then flung herself into his arms. "I love you so," she sighed. When she realized what she had said, she looked slowly up at him.

"I *do*," she said, looking adoringly at him. "And thank you so much for everything."

He framed her face between his hands. "I

have loved you from the moment I first saw you," he said, not caring that the warriors heard their confessions of love. "I would do anything for you."

Maggie's soul was touched. She hugged him again. "I don't know how it happened so quickly between us, but thank God it did," she said, tears spilling from her eyes. "Without you, I would be so alone."

"I vow to you that you will never be alone again," he said. "A man protects his wife with his soul."

"Your wife?" Maggie's breath caught, and she felt a hot flush stain her cheeks.

He smiled, then walked her to her horse and helped her into the saddle.

Their eyes held for a moment before he went and mounted his steed. The travois was attached behind him. It took Maggie a moment to realize just how much her life had changed. She had found love on this journey that had turned black with death.

She took one last look at her fallen friends. She would find a way to seek vengeance for them!

"We must go now," Wind Walker said, edging his horse over closer to hers.

"Yes, I know," Maggie said quietly.

She wheeled her horse around and headed back in the direction of the village, knowing that it would be her home. She would marry Wind Walker. She would be his wife. They would even have children.

Her thoughts helped her through her sorrow, but not past it.

That would take time.

Chapter 22

O, cunning Love! With tears
thou keep'st me blind,
Lest eyes well-seeing thy foul
faults should find.
　　　　　—William Shakespeare

Maggie paced back and forth outside the lodge where her uncle's wound was being seen to.

When she heard the shaman begin to chant, Maggie froze. Was he chanting because her uncle had just died? Or was it a normal procedure to chant while medicating someone?

She resumed her pacing as she apprehensively thought about her uncle in the hands of someone other than a doctor. Though she had to admit she was grateful that someone was near to see to his health. And since she was going to be a part of Wind Walker's world, she should conform to the ways of his people. Even if that meant accepting a shaman's way of doctoring someone.

She recalled the moment she had said that

she would marry Wind Walker. She had believed that she was alone in the world. But even if her uncle survived his wounds, she knew that she still wanted to stay with Wind Walker. She could never find such a love as theirs again in her lifetime. She couldn't let it go, even if it meant that her uncle would go on to Oregon without her.

Maggie wondered if Red would try to discourage her from marrying Wind Walker. Yet she knew for certain that she was going to stay. She wanted to be his wife.

Then her thoughts went to the children at Archy's ranch. She would never forget the fear and unhappiness in their eyes that was caused by their very own father. She could hardly bear to know they were still at his mercy.

She must find a way to get them from Archy. If not, there was no hope for their future.

"Maggie?"

Wind Walker startled her. She turned just as he stepped up to her and drew her into his embrace.

"Don't tell me that he died," she said, softly clinging.

"No, he did not die," Wind Walker answered. He held her by the shoulders and eased her away from him so that they could look into each other's eyes. "Your uncle is going to be taken to a sweat lodge. Come and see him first."

"What is a sweat lodge?" she asked, relieved that Red was still alive. "Why would he be taken there?"

"The sweat lodge is very important in the ceremonial life of the Cheyenne," Wind Walker explained. "Nothing of significance is undertaken by an individual, or group, without the sweat bath and its accompanying rites, which include prayers and songs. Even the construction of the simple lodge is done according to ritual. Anyone who builds it irreverently, or abuses it in any way, will have ill luck."

"But my uncle isn't Cheyenne," Maggie said, confused. "How can it be good for him?"

"To assure his healing process," Wind Walker said. "And we must go now to your uncle, because it is important that he be taken to the sweat lodge as quickly as possible. The sooner he sweats, the sooner he will begin the true healing process."

"If it will help my uncle," Maggie said doubtfully. "Please take me to him."

"Your uncle will be at the sweat lodge for only a short time," Wind Walker said, gently taking Maggie by an elbow, ushering her toward the entryway of the shaman's tepee. "He will be there for his time, and then taken to a tepee that is being erected for him. It will be his private place for healing. Only you, my shaman, and myself will be able to enter until he is well. Little Sparrow will bring him his food."

Maggie was again humbled by Wind Walker's kindness. How could she have ever mistrusted him?

"We will go inside," Wind Walker said, holding the entrance flap aside for Maggie. "My shaman has left to see to the arrangements at the sweat lodge. Go, Maggie. You will have a few private moments with your uncle before he is taken to the sweat lodge."

Maggie gazed into Wind Walker's eyes. She wanted to give him another hug, but was too anxious to see her uncle. She smiled, then stepped past Wind Walker into the shaman's lodge.

She stopped, struck at how pale her uncle was and how quietly he lay on a pallet of furs on his side. His eyes were closed, his lips were a purplish hue. His wound was visible to Maggie.

She saw that it had some sort of white poultice spread over it. Thankfully, the blood had been washed away.

She went and knelt down beside him. She was glad to see that he seemed to be resting comfortably.

"Red, you are going to be all right," Maggie murmured as she brushed his red hair back from his brow, then leaned low and kissed him there.

His skin was cool to the touch. She was glad that he wasn't feverish.

She sat away from him again, her eyes watching his, hoping they would open. "I'll be glad when you wake up so that we can talk. Only then, when you can tell me that you are all right, will I truly believe it."

She reached for one of his hands. "Soon you will be laughing and talking again. You'll be telling jokes and teasing me in no time."

She smiled at how he had always been a man of such good nature.

Wind Walker called her name from outside.

She gazed at her uncle again, brushed a kiss across his brow, then went outside to join Wind Walker.

Several warriors were there. A few held a stretcher that had been made from tree limbs and buckskin. Others went inside to get her uncle. They brought him outside and placed him on the stretcher. After covering him up to his chin with a blanket, they carried him away toward the river where she saw a low, dome-shaped structure with a framework of arched willow saplings.

This framework was covered with several layers of bark, earth, and grass, and even some skins and blankets. Its entrance faced the river.

A fire burned hot in a firepit close to the lodge; stones were heating in the flames.

"Come, we will sit close to the sweat lodge," Wind Walker said. He took her by the hand and followed the men and her uncle.

Maggie noticed then that the shaman came from the small lodge, his eyes old and patient as he waited for Red to be taken inside.

Maggie could not help but feel somewhat apprehensive over what was about to happen, yet she trusted Wind Walker's judgment now in all things. She knew that what was going to happen to her uncle was for his own good.

Her uncle was taken inside the lodge. After the warriors left, they waited a short distance down the river.

Wind Walker took Maggie to the opposite side, a short distance from the sweat lodge. He urged her to sit on a thick bed of moss with him.

"I shall explain as it is happening," Wind Walker said. He glanced toward the sweat lodge where Sky Dreamer was chanting and working his special magic on Red.

"A pit has been dug just inside the lodge," he said, now gazing at Maggie. "The stones that you see in the fire at the one side of the entryway will be taken inside once they are heated to red-hot. Then they will be pushed into the inside pit. Sky Dreamer will then pour water on the hot rocks. That will create the steam. Your uncle will sweat for a short while as Sky Dreamer chants songs and prayers to the spirit of the sweat lodge. The sweat bath will purify your uncle's body and propitiate the spirits to cure him."

Maggie looked toward the sweat lodge when she heard the shaman singing. He had come out and, with sticks, rolled the hot rocks inside into the pit.

She watched as the skin entrance was closed, yet she could see steam escaping from the sides of the closed flap.

She still tried to convince herself that this was good for her uncle.

She knew that this ritual had been used by Indians from the beginning of time, so surely it helped the ill.

"My shaman has poured water over the hot rocks now, bathing your uncle in its steam," Wind Walker said. "The smoke sweats out the disease. It is to cure the illness by influencing the spirits of the disease, while Sky Dreamer chants songs and prayers to the spirit of the sweat lodge."

Suddenly Maggie's eyes were drawn to the distant mountains. Her heart skipped a beat when she saw lightning flash, followed closely by the soft roll of thunder. She shuddered and hugged herself.

Coming at such a time as this, she could not help but think that a storm might be a bad omen.

She flinched when a lurid streak of lightning raced across the heavens, closer now than only moments ago.

Wind Walker saw Maggie's reaction to the thunder and lightning. He reached for her and held her in his arms. "Someday you will tell me why you are afraid of storms," he said, as her body trembled against his.

"I wasn't afraid of storms until recently," Maggie said, her voice breaking.

"Did something happen to make you afraid?"

"Yes," Maggie confessed, closing her eyes so that she couldn't see the lightning flashes. "The storms would suddenly spook the horses of the wagon train. The horses would go into a frenzy, so much that the wagons attached to them would sometimes overturn. Some of my friends were killed. It happened so often, I began to dread even the slightest sound of thunder. I knew what could happen, that I could lose more friends."

"I am sorry for your loss," Wind Walker said, his voice drawn.

"My mother died recently, too, and I feel to blame," Maggie said, her voice breaking.

"Why is that?" Wind Walker asked, searching her eyes.

Maggie told him about the snake and how quickly her mother was gone.

"It is only natural to blame oneself when one loses a loved one. I have blamed myself over so many deaths of those I loved," Wind Walker said softly. "But death comes to us because it is planned for us from the moment we are a seed in our mother's womb."

He framed Maggie's face between his hands. "My sweet, even your last moment in life, even mine, is written in the stars. It is fate. It is something that no one can change, even though our guilt makes us feel like we should have been able to. I will explain to you about one of my particular losses, but not now. Your thoughts must be with your uncle now."

He gazed heavenward, then smiled into Maggie's eyes and shifted her face so that she could look into the cloud-free sky. "Do you see?" he said softly. "There is no more lightning. There is no more thunder. It went far away into the mountains. You do not have to fear it anymore today."

Maggie saw the blue sky and white fluffy clouds, then sighed heavily with relief. She turned back to Wind Walker. "Thank you for saying the right things and doing so much for me," she said sincerely. She hugged him. "Thank you so much for caring for my uncle and seeing to his welfare."

She noticed that the chanting and singing had stopped, and looked quickly toward the small sweat lodge. Her eyes widened as the shaman came from it, smiling.

Maggie wanted to go to her uncle, but knew that she must wait until he was taken from the sweat lodge and to the new tepee that had been erected for him.

She watched as the warriors soon had him on the stretcher and were carrying him away from the river.

"Come," Wind Walker said, taking Maggie's hand. "We will go now to your uncle's tepee. You can sit beside him. Little Sparrow will bring food."

Maggie moved into his arms. "You are so wonderful."

Maggie was surprised when she turned and found the lodge being dismantled. She looked up at Wind Walker.

"A sweat lodge is used only once, then destroyed," he explained. "It has served its purpose."

She watched the shaman go inside his own personal tepee, then gazed at the tepee where her uncle had been taken.

"Go to him," Wind Walker said, motioning

with a hand toward the lodge. "Even in his sleep, he will feel your presence."

Smiling, Maggie reached a gentle hand to Wind Walker's cheek, then ran to the tepee, stepping quietly inside.

She hurried to Red's side and sat down beside him.

She reached a hand to his flushed cheek.

"I hope the sweat bath does as it is supposed to," she whispered. "By the time night comes, you should be able to sip broth from a spoon as I feed it to you."

"I would not count on that," Wind Walker said as he came into the tepee. "His sleep is deep, but restful. I do have faith that my shaman will bring good health back to your uncle, but it cannot happen as quickly as you wish it could."

Maggie started to say something but stopped when Little Sparrow came into the lodge carrying a small pot of food in one hand and a smaller pot in the other.

The wonderful aroma of cooked meat and vegetables filled the tepee, making Maggie's stomach loudly growl. A blush heated her face because she knew that both Wind Walker and Little Sparrow heard it.

"Soon the belly growls will be all gone," Little Sparrow said, setting the two pots down close to the fire.

She reached outside and fetched two wooden bowls that she had placed there earlier. She brought them into the lodge and ladled stew into them, then took two wooden spoons from a front pocket and handed one to Wind Walker and one to Maggie.

"I made this food just for you. I hope you enjoy it," Little Sparrow said. She gave Red a wavering glance. "I brought him broth. I will push the pot into the hot coals of the fire so that it will stay warm until he awakens."

"I hope that will be soon," Maggie said as she remembered Wind Walker's warning that it might take longer than she would wish.

"I will pray to *Maheo* that your uncle will be able to smile to you by nightfall," Little Sparrow said. She gave Maggie and Wind Walker hugs, then left the tepee.

"She is adorable," Maggie said. But she felt some jealousy when Wind Walker's eyes lingered on the entrance flap as it still shimmied from Little Sparrow's departure.

Wind Walker felt Maggie's eyes on him, and turned toward her. He smiled.

"You see my fondness again for Little Sparrow," he said. "Always remember, Maggie, that it is fondness I feel for her and love that I feel for you. There is quite a difference, you know."

"Yes," Maggie said, blushing. "I'm sorry if you see me as a jealous busybody."

"Busybody?" Wind Walker said, arching an eyebrow. "I have never heard that word."

Maggie giggled as she explained its meaning. Then they shared their meal, all the while Maggie glancing toward her uncle in hopes of seeing signs of him awakening.

"I want the ones who did this to my uncle to pay," Maggie said, fighting back the urge to cry again.

"In time, those who spread evil across this beautiful land will pay for their wrongful deeds," Wind Walker said. "But for now, Maggie, there are other things best thought about."

"Yes, my uncle," she said, nodding. "He has to wake up. How could a small wound cause my uncle not to recover any more quickly than he is?"

"It is the loss of blood that is to blame," Wind Walker softly explained. "Give it time. I know that your uncle will be all right. Right now, he is resting. Sometimes that is better than medicine. As he sleeps, his body is healing."

"You always say the right thing." Maggie smiled. "I don't see how I ever doubted you. But I guess it is only normal. Everyone in my community learned to fear the red man from childhood on. I always wondered why it had to be that way. There were evil white men, as well. The likes of Archy is a good example. So why do white people have to single out the red man to hate?" Maggie recalled Jeremy and Kevin. "If you could have heard the children talking about their own father and how mean he is, you would know that he is capable of anything."

"Most definitely," Wind Walker said, his voice dry and drawn.

"The children." Maggie paled at the thought of them still being at the ranch and at the mercy of their father. "It isn't fair to leave them there. We must find a way to get them."

She reached a hand to Wind Walker's arm. "You saved me. Can we save them?"

"Yes, we will save the children," he said, nodding. "But first, careful plans must be made."

When Red seemed to choke in his sleep, Maggie rushed from Wind Walker's side to check on him. She sat down and felt his brow. He was all right now, and peacefully sleeping.

"I do worry about the children," she said, giving Wind Walker a glance over her shoulder. "But for now, my uncle comes first. I cannot leave him for any reason, not until he is awake and I know he is going to be all right."

Wind Walker scooted over and slipped his arm around her waist. He drew her next to him as they both sat and watched and listened.

Chapter 23

Dear friend, far off, my lost desire,
So far, so near in woe and weal;
O loved the most, when most I feel,
There is a lower and a higher.
                    —Alfred, Lord Tennyson

A day and a night had passed since Red had gone through the sweat lodge ritual. Maggie sat beside him now, gazing worriedly at him. He was still in a deep sleep. She had scarcely left him for any amount of time after he had been brought to the tepee.

She waited anxiously for signs of him waking, yet he still slept.

She was beginning to believe that he might never wake up, although Wind Walker had said that more patience than she had ever had before was required now. He believed that her uncle would wake up soon and that he would be well.

Maggie kept trying to believe what Wind Walker had said. She wanted to think positively at a time in her life when so much had been taken from her. Yet the longer her uncle lay there, the more she doubted that she would ever talk with him again. She expected her uncle to take his final breath. Red was the last of her immediate family, and without him she would feel empty.

Yet there was Wind Walker. He had brought so much into her life at a time when she had truly felt that life could never be good again. From their first moment together he had done everything for her.

"Uncle Patrick," she whispered. "Please wake up. I have so much to tell you."

But Red still lay there, not showing any response to her voice.

Just how long could a person stay asleep like that? Maggie wondered.

"Red." She placed a gentle hand on his cheek. "Can you hear me? I'm here for you. I love you, Red."

She sighed heavily and slid her hand away from him, then slowly twined her fingers together in her lap. "Oh, Red, please, wake up."

She allowed her mind to drift elsewhere—to Archy's children. Although she was terribly anxious about her uncle, she could not stop worrying about the two motherless boys.

What was to become of Jeremy and Kevin?

Since she had been there sitting with her

uncle, Wind Walker had come into the tepee only long enough to check on her uncle, or to bring food. He had his own daily activities to see to, especially the welfare of his ailing chief. But Maggie needed his reassurance again. In truth, she hungered for him.

But she didn't ask him to stay. He was an important man in his village. He would one day be chief. He held himself in that noble way powerful chiefs held themselves. He had the love and respect of all of the people of his clan.

She closed her eyes and envisioned him as chief. . . .

"Sweet Magpie?"

That voice, that nickname, made Maggie's heart skip a beat, and her eyes snapped open. Her uncle was smiling at her, saying the name Magpie again.

"Red!" she cried, leaning low and embracing him. She sobbed with joy. "Oh, Red, I was so afraid you were not going to wake up. But you have. You're going to be all right."

"I'll be fine," Red said as she moved away from him, her tear-filled eyes taking him in. He slowly looked around. "Where are we? What happened?"

"We are in a Cheyenne village," Maggie said softly. "We are in Wind Walker's village. This tepee was made especially for you and me. He brought you here. His shaman has seen to your wound." She smiled. "And I'll tell you later about the ritual that was performed to ensure that you would survive."

Red smiled crookedly. "Yes, maybe it's best you tell me later," he said, his voice fading. He reached for Maggie's hands and took them in his. "What of the others? Did anyone else survive?"

Maggie's throat went dry. She lowered her eyes.

"No, Red," she said, her voice breaking. "No one else survived."

Red quickly averted his eyes and swallowed hard.

"Maggie, that man Archy? The cattle baron?" he said, looking into her eyes again. "Maggie, he came with renegades and ambushed us. He . . . he . . . is the one who shot me."

"I know," she said softly.

Red found it difficult to believe that he was the sole survivor, yet grateful that he had been saved. "Please find Wind Walker for me."

"He will be so glad to see that you are all right. I'll go now." She leaned over and kissed her uncle on a cheek, then rose to her feet. "I won't be long."

Maggie was elated that she had her uncle back again. He was truly on the road to recovery. She couldn't wait to share the news with Wind Walker.

She rushed from the tepee and found him standing beside the river. Her heart started to pound at the very sight of him.

Now that her uncle was going to be all right, she and Wind Walker could proceed with their future. Soon they could speak their vows. Maggie broke into a run.

When she got only a few feet away, he turned to see her. She ran to him and flung herself into his arms.

"Red is awake!" she cried. "He is going to be all right!"

Seeing her excitement, Wind Walker smiled. He was glad to hear that her uncle was awake. But he was more glad to know that Maggie could now focus on their future.

"Wind Walker," Maggie sighed. His lips kissed hers so sweetly, her knees almost buckled beneath her.

When he drew his lips away, they gazed momentarily into each other's eyes. He smiled and took her by a hand and hurried away from the river.

"It is good to see you happy," Wind Walker said, smiling down at her. "I told you that while he slept he was healing. Soon he will leave his bed."

Maggie's smile waned. "Yes, and . . . and . . . I do not know if he will want to continue his journey to Oregon, or give it up," she said. She looked up at Wind Walker. "I hate to think of him going anywhere while I stay here. You see, he is my only living relative."

"He will need to make a choice, a choice that you must accept," Wind Walker said. He stopped and placed his hands on her shoulders and turned her to face him. "Just as you have made your decision to stay with me. He is a man who will want his own future. Whatever he decides, will you be all right with it?"

"I would miss him terribly, but I know that my place is with you," Maggie answered. "He will decide what will be best for him. I just want his happiness."

"Come on." Maggie took Wind Walker by the hand. "Let's go and talk with my uncle."

When they reached the tepee, Maggie stepped ahead of Wind Walker and held back the buckskin flap for him. As he walked past her, she heard her uncle happily call Wind Walker's name and thank him.

She went and sat down beside Wind Walker as he and her uncle continued to talk about what had happened. Her uncle continued to express his gratitude over and over. It was obvious to Maggie that they respected each other.

"I'm starved," Red said as he slowly sat up, wincing momentarily as pain shot through his wound. He pulled a blanket up around his shoulders. "Yep, I'm hungry."

"That's a good sign." Maggie smiled.

She kissed Wind Walker, then Red, before leaving the tepee to fetch Little Sparrow. She wanted to share the news about her uncle and get some food. Little Sparrow always seemed to be cooking.

Maggie ran into Little Sparrow's lodge and hugged her. "My uncle is awake!" she cried. "And he's hungry."

"I am anxious to meet this man that you love so much," she said, smiling as both she and Maggie took the heavy pot of stew from the tripod over the fire.

"You will adore him," Maggie said, beaming.

Chapter 24

Known and unknown; human, divine;
Sweet human hand and lips and eye;
Dear heavenly friend that canst not die,
Mine, mine, for ever, ever mine.
            —Alfred, Lord Tennyson

A rumble of thunder in the distance warned of a storm lingering over the mountains. Maggie shivered. Yet it had not come with its fierce lightning to the Cheyenne village. For now Maggie would forget about it.

The fire in the firepit of Red's tepee was burning steadily, the orange glow of the ashes casting its soft light on Red and Wind Walker.

Wind Walker sat on one side of Red's bed of pelts as Maggie sat on the other.

Maggie smiled as she watched her uncle eating. She was so glad that the color had returned to his cheeks, his lips.

She would never forget that first time she had seen him after he had been shot, when his lips were a bluish hue.

And now he was giving her occasional smiles between sips of broth made from meat and wild fruit.

Though he was smiling, there was something lacking. Maggie understood. He now had another pain to cope with. He had to get through the shock of losing so many of his friends on the wagon train. It was supposed to have been an exciting beginning of a new life for them all in Oregon.

Now only a few of their friends had survived—the ones who had been sent ahead in case there was an ambush.

Maggie got choked up every time she thought of those who were killed. It was because of her that they had died. They had wanted to find her before resuming their journey. She had a sharp stab of guilt every time she thought about it.

But she kept reminding herself that had she been taken on to the wagon train after Wind Walker rescued her instead of to his village, she, too, might have died.

"I would like to leave today and catch up with the wagon train," Maggie said suddenly, drawing both her uncle's and Wind Walker's eyes to her. She looked from Red to Wind Walker.

"Even if the surviving members of the wagon train arrived at a fort, they have no proof of what Archy did to me," she reasoned.

"Without evidence, surely the authorities can't do anything about it."

She swallowed hard as she shoved the wooden plate of half-eaten food away. "*I am* that proof," she said stiffly. "Let's go, Wind Walker. I want Archy and the others to get their comeuppance.

"We have to do something quickly. I am not only concerned about the people on the wagon train. I am also worried about Archy's children. Each day that they are with that madman, their lives are in danger," Maggie insisted.

"There are better ways to get vengeance against a man such as Archy," Wind Walker said. "It would make things too easy just to have the authorities deal with him."

"But the children," Maggie argued. "We must think of *them*. We must get them."

"My plan will put them first," Wind Walker said. "He is a greedy man and will do anything to get what he wants. Killing seems to be his answer to everything."

"What are you thinking of doing?" Red asked, setting aside his empty bowl.

Wind Walker looked at Red. "I know of ways that will hurt him more than prison or even death."

"What are you referring to?" Maggie asked hesitantly.

"We will slowly take Archy's worldly possessions from him," Wind Walker stated. "He will eventually be left with nothing."

"How?" Maggie asked, raising an eyebrow.

"One by one he will lose what is precious to him," Wind Walker answered.

"But the children?"

"They are the first of the man's possessions that will be taken," Wind Walker said, slowly smiling.

"But Wind Walker, he doesn't see his children as precious," Maggie warned. "He will not care if they are taken from him."

"Yes, he will," Wind Walker said. "He sees them as a possession. If he does not get angry over having them taken from him because he loves them, he will most certainly get angry because they are something he owns."

"Yes, I see," Maggie said, nodding. "I believe you are right."

"What are you going to do to get this plan in motion?" Red asked, slowly laying back down, exhausted from sitting up. He groaned when the wound on his back made contact with the blankets and pelts beneath him.

"I will meet in council with the warriors," Wind Walker said, helping Red turn on his side. "We will make plans."

"I want to be involved," Maggie said. "I have quite a score to settle with that man. Please let me help."

"You are only a woman," Wind Walker said, immediately realizing his error by the anger that suddenly flashed in Maggie's eyes.

Red chuckled. "My little Magpie might be a woman, but she is very skilled at riding horses. And she can shoot to kill if she needs to," he said. "I taught her well. I wanted her to be able to defend herself on the journey West. You should let her go with you. She will prove herself."

Wind Walker gazed at Maggie. She was so tiny, so fragile, so much a woman, yet he, too, had seen her many strengths.

"Yes, Maggie, you can join us," Wind Walker said, as he gave her a knowing smile. "Yes, you are woman, but you are as courageous and valiant as any warrior who wishes to avenge what has been taken from him."

"Thank you." Maggie's pride was soothed.

She wanted him to know that she did have a tough side. She knew the importance of being a capable woman in this wild, untamed country, as well as being delicately feminine.

"I wish I could join you," Red said, his voice drawn. "But I know that I am too weak. I might have several weeks of recuperating ahead of me."

"You will be fit as a fiddle soon," Maggie said, taking one of his hands, squeezing it affectionately. "I will see to that."

Tears filled Red's eyes. "My *friends*. I wish they had been as fortunate as me and Maggie. But . . ."

"They have been given a proper burial," Maggie said, feeling a stab of guilt that neither she nor a preacher had been able to speak over the graves.

"Your friends are now among the stars," Wind Walker said softly.

"How beautiful," Maggie said, her eyes looking into Wind Walker's.

There was a sudden large, lurid flash of lightning that lit up the whole interior of the tepee, followed soon by a loud clap of thunder.

Maggie got up and rushed around the fire to fling herself into Wind Walker's arms. Trembling, she clung to him.

Red saw the same fierce fear that storms had been causing in Maggie since the deaths of some of their friends due to spooked horses. But something else caught his attention. She had gone to Wind Walker for comfort instead of to him.

He had seen their affection for each other and wondered just how far it had gone. When they looked at each other, it was evident to Red how much they cared for each other. Was it love?

Maggie had never been in love before. Had she chosen a red man over white after so many fine, even rich, gentlemen in Boston had wanted to court her? Red worried that it was intrigue or infatuation.

He just wanted her happiness. If she chose Wind Walker because he made her happy, who was Red to argue about it?

"There is a cure for this fear of storms," Wind Walker said quietly, while stroking her back.

"There is?" she asked softly, her eyes searching his.

"Do you want to be cured?" Wind Walker asked, returning her steady gaze.

Red started to interrupt. "I'm not sure . . ."

"My shaman cured you," Wind Walker said as he gazed over at Red. "Now he will cure your niece. Then council will be held to make plans about Archy. The Ute renegades will be dealt with later, for they, too, are responsible for the deaths of your friends and many, many others."

Red sighed heavily. "I trust you, Wind Walker. I trust your shaman."

Maggie turned and bent low to hug her uncle. "I do too," she whispered against his cheek, then turned back to Wind Walker and held a hand out for him. "Please take me to Sky Dreamer. If you say that I can be cured, then I shall be."

She gave her uncle another smile. Then, just

as she stepped outside with Wind Walker, rain began falling from the sky in sheets so hard the drops stung Maggie's flesh.

The lightning and thunder were so fierce and constant, she wanted to scream. She clung more tightly to Wind Walker's hand as they ran now toward the shaman's tepee, yet her whole insides were quivering.

She was relieved when they reached the shaman's lodge, where for a while, at least, she would be inside and safely away from the wrath of nature.

As Wind Walker held the entrance flap aside, Maggie rushed inside, Wind Walker following after her.

The elderly shaman was sitting beside his lodge fire, his head bent in sleep, his dark robe of bearskin picking up the light of the flames, making him look mysterious.

Now that she was there, Maggie's heart raced. She wondered about the wisdom of her decision. How could anyone have the power to take away fear? It seemed somehow connected with the supernatural and that frightened her.

But she trusted Wind Walker's judgments, and therefore, she would trust him in this, too. If there was a chance that this elderly man could help her, she would take it.

"Sit," Wind Walker said, gesturing with a hand toward the thick pelts beside Sky

Dreamer. His deep-timbered voice woke the shaman, who was now gazing questioningly at both of them.

Wind Walker sat on Maggie's other side, and quickly explained to Sky Dreamer about Maggie's fears.

"I have brought her to you for your cure," Wind Walker said. He wanted Maggie's fear of storms to be cured, but at the same time Wind Walker hoped to rid himself of the awful memories that thunderstorms brought of the day his wife died.

"Do you believe that what I will do will cure you?" Sky Dreamer asked, his old eyes studying Maggie. "One must believe, or it will not happen."

Again, Maggie could not help but be skeptical, but she reminded herself again that she trusted Wind Walker. She would put her entire trust in his shaman now.

"Yes, I believe." She nodded. "Please help me."

"Wind Walker, go and fetch my *wanowah*, medicine bag," Sky Dreamer said, gesturing with a bony hand toward a bag at the left side of his lodge.

Wind Walker did as he asked. Maggie watched as the shaman reached inside the bag and took out something wrapped in buckskin. She breathlessly waited for Sky Dreamer to do whatever he was going to do with the bag, and felt apprehension rise within her.

"This medicine is used for curing many things, but especially fear of storms," Sky Dreamer said. "You will notice that this is doubly wrapped. The inside wrapping is of a heart covering, which is hard and tough. The outer covering is of buckskin. I will take it outside with me as I perform the ritual that will help you."

Maggie felt strange about it, but made herself remember that almost everything she experienced at the Cheyenne village would be different from what she had known. She knew the importance of accepting and learning all of Wind Walker's world.

"Come with me outside," Sky Dreamer said, groaning with the effort it took for him to stand. Wind Walker hurried to him and helped him.

Maggie trembled as she waited just inside the entryway, as Wind Walker helped the elderly man past her.

Wind Walker stepped back into the tepee. He held her for a moment, whispering encouraging words into her ear. Then he smiled down at her and held her hand as he led her outside into the storm.

Maggie still trembled. Her heart raced. Her knees were weak as lightning flashed and thunder roared all around her. Her face was wet anew from the rain falling on it.

"Watch and feel!" Sky Dreamer said.

He stood away from both Wind Walker and Maggie and began talking to the thunder, the rain sliding down his leathery, old face.

Maggie was in awe of the sudden strength of his body. He no longer needed to be helped by Wind Walker. Sky Dreamer went back inside his lodge carrying the bundle, then came out again. He repeated this process four times, each time facing one of the four directions as he talked to the thunder.

Maggie listened and noticed that Sky Dreamer did not ask the thunder to take pity on *her*, but instead, demanded that it come on down from the sky and kill *him*.

The lightning flashes seemed to draw nearer. The ground beneath Maggie's feet trembled fiercely as the thunder roared and grumbled all around her.

After the shaman requested four times to be killed by the lightning, and it did not happen, Maggie suddenly felt no fear. Her body ceased its constant tremors. Her heart did not pound like an extension of the thunder inside her chest.

She felt free. She felt at peace! Her fear had been taken away.

Wind Walker felt his own sudden freedom

inside his heart. Without having to ask his shaman to include him in this special ceremony, he felt his unrest was removed. He wanted to cry out to the heavens that his demons had been defeated and washed away, yet he knew the importance of this being Maggie's time, so he stood aside and watched her run into the rain and laugh as thunder boomed all around her.

"I am no longer afraid. I fear nothing!" she cried. "I am free! Free!"

Wind Walker turned to thank his shaman, but he was back inside his lodge already, surely feeling blessed, himself, to know that he still had powers that he had had as a young man.

Wind Walker wanted to go in and thank him, but knew that this was a private time of prayer for Sky Dreamer, which he needed after any ceremony. Instead, Wind Walker joined Maggie, laughing along with her, his face held heavenward as the rain continued to splash onto it.

As the storm ceased and the sky turned a sparkling blue, Wind Walker drew Maggie fully up into his arms and kissed her. He leaned away and smiled into her eyes.

"My woman, I have a place that I want you to see," he said. "Will you go with me?"

"Wind Walker, don't you know that I would go anywhere with you?" Maggie responded breathlessly. "Thank you for what just happened. It worked. I will never fear storms again!"

"Then you will not fear what I am about to show you," he said, smiling. "Come. Let me take you there."

She took his hand, curious as to where he was taking her. But once again, she put her full trust in him.

Chapter 25

What art thou then? I cannot guess;
But tho' I seem in star and flower
To feel thee some diffusive power,
I do not therefore love thee less.
            —Alfred, Lord Tennyson

The storm had passed, and the ground steamed as Wind Walker held Maggie's hand as they walked down to the river. He led her along the riverbank until the village was no longer in view, nor the smoke that spiraled slowly from the tepees.

Maggie was tempted to ask him where he was taking her, but knew that he must have a special reason.

As they walked toward the remains of a burnt willow tree, Maggie glanced at Wind Walker. She saw many things hanging from the scorched limbs of the tree. They looked to be gifts of some sort.

"I wanted you to see a place where lightning and thunder left an imprint inside my heart forever. Only moments ago, when my shaman took the fear from your heart, he also erased the ache that was left inside me," he said, stopping only inches from it. "This is where my wife died. Lightning came from the heavens and struck the tree. She was kneeling too close as she was washing her hair in the river. She and the tree died because of the lightning, the thunder vibrating in the very ground her silent body fell upon."

He gazed into Maggie's eyes. "I know that you have recently lost loved ones," he said. "Maggie, spirits are everywhere in nature. Spirits make the grass and plants grow. Spirits cause the winds to blow and the clouds to float across the sky. Spirits remain on earth when the body dwindles away to nothingness.

"Every animal and bird has a spirit. The spirits of those you love are with you always. They embrace the wind that blows around you. They are in the flowers that you look upon in the springtime. They *are* the flowers. They *are* the wind. What I am saying, my love, even though you no longer see their physical presence, their spirit never dies.

"You recently lost your parents. They are with you even now in your heart. It is in this way that they will never leave you. My wife, too, is inside my heart, and in that respect will never leave me. But she smiles because she knows that I have found someone, you, to fill that ache in my heart that was left there by her death. Her spirit is now in the heavens, as are your parents'. They know that I am here to protect and love you. You can let go, too, for where they are is a far better place than earth."

"No place could ever be more wonderful for me than where I am now, Wind Walker," Maggie said. "For I am with you."

Wind Walker untied a small buckskin bag that hung from his belt, then knelt down before the tree with it. He kissed the tiny bag before tying it to a limb, then gazed heavenward and said a quiet prayer.

Once he was finished, he stood and turned to Maggie. His eyes searched hers. "My devotion is still strong to my first wife, yet it now shifts to you," he said with meaning. "She is of my past. You are of my future. I will be the best of husbands to you."

He drew her into his embrace. She twined her arms around his neck as he lowered his lips to hers and gave her an endearing kiss, one that made her heart sing with happiness.

Suddenly he swept her into his arms. "I have another place that I would like to show you," he said huskily. "It is a place where I have gone to contemplate life, to look at things of beauty, to marvel over the goodness nature has to offer.

I wish to share this special place with you. I wish to make love with you there."

Maggie's eyes widened. She swallowed hard at the thought of making love for the first time in her life. But she wasn't married. She had always been told by her mother that making love before marriage was a sin.

Maggie pushed her mother's admonishments aside. She loved Wind Walker. She would not waste another moment thinking that it was wrong to be together in such a way. She *was* going to marry Wind Walker when they could find the proper time to do so.

Right now, there was so much that needed to be done. It did not matter that they postponed the marriage until everything else was taken care of. Lives depended on them. Especially those two innocent children whose father was the devil incarnate.

As Wind Walker continued carrying Maggie, her heart started to race faster. She hoped that she would be skilled enough at lovemaking so that he would not be disappointed in her. She clung to his neck and counted out the moments with each of his footsteps.

Finally he stopped and she looked around at what had to be paradise on earth.

There was a slight waterfall making gentle splashes in the water below. Rainbows arched in the air above it. Blue flowers were draped around the trees along the riverbank. Beautiful, thick ferns were everywhere, entwined with a colorful mixture of autumn flowers.

Overhead, the autumn leaves on the trees were like a patchwork quilt in their varied colors. Nearby, small plants with tiny white flowers sent off the sweetest fragrance. The fragrance could match any of the fanciest of French perfumes.

Maggie recognized the smell. It resembled the lily of the valley plants that had grown outside her mother's bedroom window in the spring. It was her mother's favorite flower.

But this was now, and Maggie was with the man with whom she was going to spend the rest of her life.

When he gazed down at her, she smiled adoringly into his eyes.

"It is so beautiful here," she sighed.

"A reflection of you," Wind Walker said, his eyes revealing the depth of his love for her. "You are the loveliest woman I have ever seen—and you are mine."

"Yes, I am yours," Maggie answered. "Forever and a lifetime."

Then she blushed and lowered her eyes, suddenly feeling bashful in this mighty man's presence. "You make me feel special," she murmured as she placed a gentle hand on his cheek. "I love you, Wind Walker."

"I know," he said huskily, the heat of his eyes scorching. "I can feel it deep inside my soul. And I love you."

His lips came to hers again, meltingly hot and filled with a passion that was new to Maggie. It made everything within her cry out for him, yearning for more. She ached where she had never known she even had feelings before. All of her senses were ignited.

She let out a soft cry as he slid a hand up inside the buckskin dress and found her secret place where no man's hand had ever been before. He began stroking her, waking dormant feelings inside her. Her body felt delicious and wonderful. She gave herself up to the rapture.

She was so overwhelmed by the new feelings, she was scarcely aware that he had lowered her to the ground on a thick bed of luscious soft moss.

His kisses and caresses were intoxicating. She was unaware of him undressing her, his clothes quickly following hers.

Suddenly he was there, his nakedness blanketing her own, his body outstretched over hers, his manhood probing. She willingly opened herself up to him, holding her legs out to make it easier for him to move within her.

His heat penetrated her. Her tightness slowly unfolded to him. She clung to his neck as he kissed her.

She cried out against his lips as he broke through the barrier that proved she was a virgin.

He kissed her with a fierce, possessive heat, and soon the momentary pain changed into wondrous bliss. Slowly he began moving in her.

A raging hunger flooded her senses. She groaned in ecstasy as his lean, sinewy buttocks moved. His lips captured one of her breasts, his tongue flicking around her nipple.

Wind Walker's body was growing feverish. Her body was like a sweet elixir to his wounded soul.

"My beautiful Maggie," he whispered against her lips, his hand filled with one of her tiny round breasts.

Currents of warmth swept through him as he kissed her. He moved slowly within her, yet with acute deliberation.

"I never knew love could be this wonderful, or that this would be so divine," Maggie whispered back to him, her eyes closed.

Her insides quivered as his body moved rhythmically against hers, the heat of his manhood thrusting within her.

"We have a lifetime of loving ahead of us," Wind Walker whispered. His face flushed hot from the building ecstasy, he brushed soft kisses across her lips.

Maggie sighed, then sucked in a wild breath of rapture as he quickened his strokes. He kissed her again with passionate heat.

She twined her legs around him so he could fill her more deeply. She seemed almost beyond coherent thought, the pleasure was so intense.

She gasped as he sucked on one nipple then the other, before licking his way down to her belly, withdrawing his manhood from inside her.

His tongue trailed lower until he reached the juncture of her thighs, where he began flicking his tongue across her womanhood, bringing sheer ecstasy to the surface.

She tossed her head back and forth.

She twined her fingers through his thick black hair to press his lips closer to her. Maggie cried out as her world seemed to explode into a million pieces.

Then his manhood was filling her again.

She was breathless and still slightly stunned, but she didn't have time to think about it.

As he thrust into her, over and over again, that same delicious feeling that she had only moments ago experienced began to build again, flooding her entire being with an intense pleasure.

Wind Walker wrapped his arms around her waist and pulled her even more closely to him and closed his eyes. He pressed his cheek against her breasts and gritted his teeth as one last plunge within her brought him that same blissful explosion she had experienced twice before. He spilled his seed inside her warm and wonderful place, his body lurching over and over again until he was spent.

He moved his lips to hers, kissing her gently. He whispered to her as he withdrew his manhood and moved his hand there to gently stroke her. He could feel her breath catch each time he touched that one delicate, tender place.

"My woman, my woman," he whispered huskily.

"My beautiful Cheyenne warrior," she whispered back, her hands stroking his buttocks, her body relaxed and fulfilled from the ecstasy she had just shared with the man she would always love and adore.

Chapter 26

Far off thou art, but ever nigh;
I have thee still, and I rejoice;
I prosper, circled with thy voice;
I shall not lose thee tho' I die.
          —Alfred, Lord Tennyson

The moon was bright and high in the sky as Maggie rode with Wind Walker and his men toward Archy's ranch.

The council had been brief, but accurate in their planning. The Golden Eagle Clan's plans were to take swift action tonight and show their strength.

Dressed in men's clothes, to make travel easier for her and to better blend in with the men, Maggie felt trepidation about tonight's activities. She was proud to be a part of it, yet couldn't help feeling some fear. She had never done anything as daring or dangerous as this.

The plan was to cause a stampede to draw Archy and his men away from the house so that the children could be taken. The fact that the children would finally be away from their tyrant father overrode her fear. And the fact that she would have a role in Archy's comeuppance was worth any danger she was putting herself in.

Her spine stiffened as the sound of the longhorns groaning carried through the night air, reminding Maggie of the time she was forced to spend at Archy's house. They were getting closer to the longhorns and Archy's homesteaded property.

"My brothers, now is the time to watch for those hired to guard the longhorns because we are nearing where they graze!" Wind Walker shouted as he gazed over his shoulder at the warriors. "Silence the white men however you must, just be certain none are left to stop our plan!"

His men silently nodded.

Wind Walker turned to Maggie as they rode onward. "Now is the time to draw back and wait if you are afraid," he said. "I can go on to the house. I can get the children and bring them to you."

"Unless I am there, they would be too afraid to leave with you. You're an Indian," Maggie said, giving him an apologetic look as she said it.

She looked down at the buckskins she was wearing. "If they see my clothes and not my face, I, too, might have a problem rescuing them."

"So you wish to continue even though you fear that we might not be successful?" Wind Walker asked, his eyes searching hers.

"Yes, I will do everything that I can to get those children away from him," Maggie said fiercely. "But first, we have to make certain Archy is gone from the house."

"As soon as he hears the thunder of his longhorns' hooves against the earth as they run in desperation, he will leave his house to try to stop them," Wind Walker said. "As soon as he leaves the house, we shall enter. By the time he reaches his longhorns, there will be no way he can stop them. He will lose much of his herd tonight, as well as his children."

Maggie nodded at Wind Walker before turning her focus back to the task at hand. The longhorns were becoming restless from the arriving horses. Maggie could see them beneath the light of the moon. They were tossing their heads high in the air, bellowing, and nervously swishing their tails back and forth.

She looked guardedly around for any signs of cowhands, finding it strange that thus far she had not seen any. They encountered more longhorns that did not seem all that disturbed by the approaching warriors.

Maggie gave Wind Walker a quick glance

when she saw several longhorns becoming aware of the intruders. The steers were just now stirring.

"Shouldn't we hurry so that the warriors can start the stampede?" Maggie asked, her heart pounding as the moment to risk everything to save the children was almost at hand.

She looked over at the longhorns again. She realized that the air was charged with tension. Another steer rose and stood rigidly still, expectant.

Wind Walker nodded at Maggie. "It is time to break away from my warriors and ride hard toward the house."

He was puzzled that none of Archy's cowhands had become alerted to what was happening. He hadn't seen any. No one came from the bunkhouse that sat close enough to the grazing pastures so that they would be the first to hear the commotion among the longhorns.

Maggie slapped her reins hard against her horse's rump. She sank her moccasined heels into its flanks and lay low over the horse as she sent it into a hard gallop. Her eyes flicked from side to side and then ahead as she waited for someone to spy her and Wind Walker gaining on the house.

Still, she saw no one.

But she heard what was happening behind

her. The pounding hooves of the longhorns popped and clicked while horns clacked upon horns in the animals' desperation to flee from the warriors. She looked over her shoulder and saw the longhorns picking up speed and scattering in all directions.

"There is Archy!" Wind Walker warned. "Maggie, get to cover quickly. Follow me. As soon as Archy is out of sight, we will go for the children!"

Maggie followed Wind Walker and breathed hard as she hid in the shadows of the tall barn with him. Squinting, she tried to see Archy, but instead could only see the crazed longhorns in the distance.

There was a buzzing noise now, loud and deafening as the longhorns stopped and crowded and milled together, their heads jammed together, their horns locked.

They broke apart as Archy came chasing and yelling at them, his rope flying.

"The warriors have done their duty and will leave and wait for us at a place I designated," Wind Walker said. "Archy will be busy enough not to notice what is happening at his house. Now we can get the children!"

As they rode toward the house, Maggie looked over her shoulder and could see Archy zigzagging in front of the longhorns, trying to direct their course. But he had no control.

The rushing mob of longhorns were at each other's heels, propelled by its own mass, plunging over the hesitating leaders. Some fell. The herd piled up, and the animals on the bottom were trampled.

The animals were stampeding without direction, some cattle trying to run in a circle, bunches cutting off this way and that.

She smiled as she got another look of Archy in the distance, and then saw some cowhands who had probably been caught off guard in the bunkhouse and had finally joined him.

Archy had managed to gain some control as he circled around the longhorns and led them back inside the fence closer to the house, then rode off again in attempt to round up some others.

"We must hurry," Wind Walker said, running inside the house with Maggie.

Her heart pounding, she ran down a dark corridor to the end, where she knew the children should be sleeping.

Jeremy came from the bedroom, his eyes wide. "Maggie!" he cried, flinging himself into her arms as she knelt down. "I was woke up by the longhorns. Just as I looked outside I saw you ride up with the Indian." He leaned back and gazed at how she was dressed. "Why are you dressed like that? Why are you with an Indian?"

"I'll tell you all about it later," Maggie promised, reaching a hand out for Kevin as he, too, ran to her. "All you need to know now is that Wind Walker and I have come to take you away from here. Do you want to go?"

"Oh, please take us," Jeremy cried. "Please, please . . ."

"Will you trust Wind Walker enough to let him carry you?" Maggie asked Kevin, her eyes pleading as the moon came through a window, bright and clear on her face.

"If he is your friend, yes, I will go with him," Kevin said solemnly. "Are we going to an Indian village?"

"Yes, where everyone is friendly," Maggie said, lifting Jeremy into her arms as Wind Walker lifted Kevin, both boys still in their pajamas and barefoot.

"Hurry now," Wind Walker said, his eyes ever watching for movement in the dark, unsure if someone was left in the house to stop him and Maggie's flight with the children.

They ran outside with the children and were soon on their horses and riding away from the ranch house. They rode in a wide circle that took them far enough from where the longhorns had been so that Archy couldn't see them.

"You children are free now," Maggie said, feeling able to talk now that they were riding across land far from the homestead. "You can start a new life."

Jeremy suddenly sobbed as he clung to her from his seat in front of her.

"Why are you crying?" Maggie asked, drawing Jeremy's eyes up to her.

"Pa was mean, but still he's our pa," he said, his voice breaking. "I feel mean leaving him like this."

Maggie was momentarily stunned, yet Archy *was* his father. It seemed only right that the boys might have second thoughts about abandoning him. But Maggie was sure that once they realized the full extent of being away from their tyrant father, they would feel relief. Jeremy and Kevin could finally have a life where they no longer had to cower in the presence of adults, where they did not have to fear the razor strop against their tiny backs.

"Things will be all right," Maggie reassured softly. "Just you wait and see. You will have many friends, and you can play games with them. You can learn to hunt with them. Has your father ever taken you on a hunt?"

"No," Jeremy said, his voice catching again.

"Well, then, see?" Maggie encouraged. "You will be doing the things that boys are supposed to do."

"Will you be taking me to where there are other white boys?" Jeremy asked, his eyes wide.

"In time, if that is what you wish," Maggie assented. "But for now you will be going to the Indian village where you will be safe."

"I'm tired," Jeremy said, yawning. He snuggled more closely against Maggie. "Thank you, Maggie. Thank you for not forgetting me and my brother."

"I never could have forgotten you," Maggie said, her voice drawn. "From the moment I left the ranch I began thinking of ways to get you."

"And you did," Jeremy said, drifting off to sleep against her.

She slid a protective arm around him, then gazed over at Wind Walker and saw that Kevin, too, was asleep.

Just ahead they saw the warriors waiting for them. When the warriors saw Maggie and Wind Walker approaching, they came to meet them.

"How did it go?" Wind Walker asked Blue Wing as he edged his horse over closer to Wind Walker's.

"It is strange how we had no one fighting against us," Blue Wing said, shrugging. "I did not see any men until I saw Archy riding from his ranch. Then my brothers and I rode into the cover of trees and onward until we arrived here to wait for you."

"Cowhands finally joined him," Wind Walker said. "But not many."

"Yes, but did you notice that they only tried to redirect the longhorns back inside a fence?" Maggie asked.

"Perhaps some realized Archy's evilness and did not want to be blamed for his actions so fled to safety," Wind Walker suggested.

"They are the smart ones," Maggie said, smiling over at Wind Walker. "I wonder what Archy thinks about them abandoning him? I imagine he is fit to be tied."

"It is just the beginning of his downfall," Wind Walker said knowingly. "One thing at a time will be taken from him until he has nothing left."

"That can't happen soon enough," Maggie said, her eyes narrowing angrily. "Until he pays dearly for all of his sins, I won't rest. To have killed so many innocent people . . ."

"My woman, do not let those thoughts take away the victory of the moment," Wind Walker said, smiling over at her. "We achieved our first goal tonight. Tomorrow we shall achieve our second. He will wish he had never stepped on Cheyenne land."

Soon Archy would know the meaning of total defeat!

Maggie wanted to know that those who had died at his hand could rest in peace.

Chapter 27

How small a part of time they share
That are so wondrous sweet and fair!
                    —Edmund Waller

Hot, sweaty, and bone weary from having searched for hours for his lost longhorns, Archy was fuming as he paced back and forth in his study.

"Damn it all to hell," he grumbled to himself, flailing an arm in the air. "I have no idea how many I lost during that stampede, but I do know it's way too many. One more stampede could put me outta business."

Frowning, he went to the window and looked outside, toward the empty pasture where normally many longhorns grazed on the purple alfalfa.

Now even the longhorn that had always defied him with his bloodred stare and loud snorts was gone.

"How?" he cried, again pacing. "Who did this to me?"

Then he stopped again and stared at the bunkhouse through his window. He could hardly believe how many of his men had deserted him last night, and even before they were needed to help round up the cattle.

The few remaining men under his employ had seen the others leave. The men who left had been afraid of what might happen to them if someone discovered their role in the recent ambush of the wagon train and had hightailed it out of there, to parts unknown. And the few men who were left at his ranch did not seem all that trustworthy. The shifty looks in their eyes made a chill ride his spine. Although they had been threatened with their lives were they to do anything against him, they could leave, too.

"Now what am I to do?" he said. He slumped down in a plush leather chair.

He stared at the flames in his fireplace, slowly going over everything that had happened last night.

He had been awakened by the loud bellowing longhorns and the thunder of their hooves as they had started stampeding. By the time he had gotten outside and on his horse, it was already too late to catch up with most of the cattle. They had already fled far and wide.

He still couldn't figure out what had

spooked the longhorns. There had been no storm last night, the lightning sometimes a threat to the peaceful animals. He had seen more than one stampede caused by lightning. He could recall the few times when lightning had actually struck the horns of a huge brindle bull. Now, that was a sight to see.

After he and his cowhands had rounded up as many as they could, and he realized just how many of his men had abandoned the ranch, he had asked the others if it were possible that the leaving cowhands could have caused the stampede. They all swore that the men had left hours before then.

"Archy!" Cookie's voice startled Archy to his feet.

"The kids!" Cookie said, huffing and puffing as he came into the study, sweat rolling down his pudgy red cheeks. "The kids are gone, Archy. Someone must've came and took 'em."

Archy paled. "What do you mean the boys are gone?"

"I went to wake 'em to tell 'em to get dressed for breakfast," Cookie said, wringing his thick hands. "They weren't in their beds. Nor were they in their room or anywheres else. I've looked high and low for 'em. They are most certainly gone."

"Damn," Archy said, the heat of anger returning color to his cheeks.

He brushed past Cookie and hurried to the children's room. He noticed that they had slept awhile in their beds, for their quilts were askew.

Stunned that they were gone, Archy stared blankly from one bed to the other. How had they left?

He turned to Cookie as he came into the room. "Who did this?" he shouted. "Who took 'em?"

"I have no idea," Cookie said, brushing a trembling hand through the greasy ash-brown hair that hung to his shoulders, hoping that Archy couldn't tell a lie when he looked it square in the eye. The truth was that Cookie had seen the boys leaving with Maggie and Wind Walker. He had not interfered. He had been concerned about the boys' welfare for some time now.

Hoping that Maggie could give the children a better life, Cookie had stayed in the shadows and watched the kids be taken from the house, then went to a window to watch them hurry away into the dark shadows of night.

Archy hung his head. "If it ain't one thing, it's another."

He firmed his jaw and looked quickly up at Cookie. "Someone is out for my blood and knows just how to get it," he said dryly. "First my longhorns, and then my kids."

"And you've lost a lot of your cowhands," Cookie reminded. "It's not a good day for you, Archy. Not a good day at all."

"Someone is purposely doing this to get back at me," Archy fumed. "I wonder if a couple of the men who left last night decided to take the boys with them."

"I just cain't imagine any of those men having the nerve to do that," Cookie said dryly, continuing with his lie. "They had to know if they got caught, you'd beat them silly with your whip."

"Then do you think the boys took out on their own?" Archy asked, forking an eyebrow.

"Yeah, I think they might have backbone enough to do it," Cookie said, purposely trying to mislead him. "Yep. They've been unhappy since their ma died. They've been a pitiful sight to see. Anyone who saw 'em had to feel sorry for 'em."

"I can think of one person who felt sorry for them." Archy tried to think it through. "Maybe that Miss Prissy Maggie person. But she couldn't have had anything to do with it. She wouldn't dare take a chance at getting caught. And she's probably far away by now, on the wagon train that escaped."

"What are you going to do?" Cookie asked, glancing sidewise at Archy.

"Right now, even if I did have someone to

blame, I don't have enough manpower to do much of anything about it," Archy said. He went to the window and looked at the few longhorns that were left. "I need help."

He turned to Cookie. "I'm going to the Ute stronghold. They owe me a favor or two. I'm going to get their help in finding my steers and rounding them up. Then I'm going to ask them to help me find my kids."

"You're askin' for more trouble than you might bargain for if you involve those lyin', thievin' renegades in your problems again," Cookie warned. "Archy, accept your losses. Go out and round up as many steers as you can and start all over again. You know you have the knack for breeding cattle. And as for the kids? I'd forget them, too. I'd say you're better off, wouldn't you? Since their ma's death, they've been so unhappy you couldn't get much outta them 'cept whinin' and complainin'. Surely wherever they are now is better'n them bein' here at the ranch, in your way . . . and mine."

"And so that's what you think of my kids, huh?" Archy said, turning to glare at Cookie. "I thought you cared for them. But here I find out they were only a nuisance."

"Well? Weren't they?" Cookie said, still lying through his teeth, for he adored the children and would miss them.

"I have to admit it, they've been kind of a handful since their ma died," he said. "I thought that woman I brung here would change things. It did that all right. It seems all hell has broke loose since I laid my eyes on that pretty little thing's face."

"Forget 'er," Cookie said. "Forget the kids."

"For now I will," Archy said dryly. "I don't have any choice. But the Utes can still help me. I'm goin' there today. You stay behind. Keep an eye on what's left, Cookie. Both our futures depend on it."

Cookie went to the window and watched Archy ride away toward the mountains, alone. "Godspeed," he whispered to himself. "You're going to need it now, Archy. I believe it's the beginning of the end for you . . . and possibly even me."

Chapter 28

The bond of Nature draw me to my own—
My own is thee, for what thou art is mine.
                              —John Milton

Relieved to have the children away from their father, Maggie stood outside Wind Walker's lodge watching Kevin and Jeremy play with the Cheyenne children. At first, after Maggie sat with Jeremy and Kevin while they ate their breakfast beside the fire in Wind Walker's tepee, the boys had not said much. They had eaten heartily because they had not had much food since Maggie had cooked their last meal at Archy's ranch.

They ate in silence, looking as though they had not slept very well at the Indian village. Maggie had not slept much, herself, for she kept wondering what Archy would do about his missing children once he discovered they were gone.

If he thought carefully enough about it, and put two and two together, he would realize that the stampede was caused in order for someone to get the children.

After everyone had returned to the village, they started celebrating the success of their moonlight venture. However, it had been short-lived when Wind Walker had told the warriors to prepare for the possibility of Archy coming to the village. Sentries had even been doubled. When everyone was settled in for the night—the sentries at their posts, the people in their lodges—Wind Walker and Maggie had helped the children into their beds of blankets in Wind Walker's tepee.

Maggie had seen the trust in Jeremy's and Kevin's eyes when they looked at her. But she could see the fear when they gazed at Wind Walker. She had sat with them and explained how wonderfully she had been treated by the Cheyenne, especially by Wind Walker. She had even told them that he would soon be her husband.

Somehow they had accepted that reality, yet were still stiff and quiet as they scooted closely to each other beneath their blankets.

Maggie had sang a soft song to them as their eyes slowly closed, then sat with them until she knew they were fully asleep, before going to Wind Walker's bed. She slipped into his arms and found comfort and love again as they snuggled between blankets beside the fire.

Maggie's body hungered for Wind Walker's hands and lips, but knew that would have to come later. They needed to be alone, not this close to the children.

But it had been enough to just be with Wind Walker. She felt she loved him even more for caring enough for the children to risk losing some of his men to rescue them.

As she stood at the entryway now, the morning so beautiful, the autumn air crisp, her eyes were drawn to Chief Half Moon's tepee. Wind Walker was there, sitting vigil at the old chief's side. He had been summoned early in the morning and told that his chief had worsened and was asking for him.

Soon the man she loved would be a powerful chief. It was sad that Chief Half Moon must die in order to relinquish his title. But she understood all too well how uneasily death came to those who waited. Her father had died slowly and painfully after his heart attack. In the end, it had been almost a relief to see him go.

But her mother's death had come swiftly, but surely no less painfully than her father's. Surely the snakebite had been excruciatingly painful until her heart stopped beating.

Maggie shook her head in order to get such

thoughts from her mind, and instead looked at the children. They looked cute in the Indian outfits that Little Sparrow had brought to them this morning. They wore fringed breeches and shirts, as well as moccasins.

They had been hesitant at first to allow Little Sparrow to weave their long blond hair into braids down their backs. But after Little Sparrow had taken the children to the entryway and pointed out how the Cheyenne children wore their hair—the boys with one long braid, the girls two—they had agreed.

Kevin and Jeremy had finished their breakfast and were now running and laughing with the young braves their age, flying kites that were made from animal-bladder skins. Maggie became choked up with emotion. She thought this might be the first time the boys had been able to behave as children and interact with other children.

Their laughter was wonderful to hear. It was infectious, for all of the young braves were laughing as they shared their toys.

"Hey, Sweet Magpie."

She turned and found Red leaning on a stick made into the shape of a cane as he ambled slowly toward her. He limped to her. Breathing hard, he took hold of one of her arms to help steady himself.

"Red!" Maggie said, quickly grabbing him

by his other arm. "You're well enough to be out of bed?"

Her eyes swept over him and saw that, like the children, he was also wearing fringed buckskins. His red hair had been cropped back from his shoulders, and his mustache . . .

"You shaved your mustache," she gasped. Then she giggled. "Who talked you into it? Uncle Patrick, I have never seen you without a mustache."

"Sky Dreamer," Red said, chuckling. "He told me that it was not good to keep unplucked hair on one's face, that it isn't the way of the Cheyenne."

"Did you remind him that you aren't Cheyenne?" Maggie asked, her eyes dancing into his.

"No, I saw no need for that," Red said, idly shrugging. "After what these people have done for both you and me, who was I to argue over a small thing as a mustache when the shaman asked if he could pluck it off for me?"

"Pluck?" Maggie asked warily. "Do you mean . . . ?"

"Yes, hair by hair," Red said, again chuckling.

Maggie gazed closely where the mustache used to be. "There is a fine white line left there," she said as she ran a finger over the shiny white space above his lips. "How does it feel?"

"It feels odd, cold and bare," he said, smiling

his good-natured smile. "How does it look? I haven't been able to look into a mirror. Sky Dreamer says he doesn't have one. He says the river is his people's mirror."

"Do you want to go and see?" Maggie asked, taking him by a hand.

Red gazed toward the river, frowned, then shook his head. "No," he said. "I'm not quite up to that far of a walk yet. Maybe tomorrow."

He looked at Kevin and Jeremy. "How are the boys faring this morning?" he asked, then smiled. "You don't have to answer that. I see for myself. They seem to have come alive, don't they?"

"They have many years of play to catch up with," Maggie said, nodding as she watched the boys still enjoying their new friends.

The animal-bladder skin kites had been laid aside. Kevin and Jeremy were now looking at and admiring the young braves' small bows. They were each handed a bow and arrow and shown how to shoot at the low hanging leaves of the birch trees.

Maggie glanced over at the young Cheyenne girls, who were not interested in what the boys were doing. They were playing house by making little tepees of sticks and gopher skins. She envisioned having a little girl someday who would do the same. She envisioned having a son who would be shooting little arrows from little bows. She prayed to herself that hers and Wind Walker's sons would be in the exact image of their father, for she had never seen anyone as handsome as Wind Walker.

Again she gazed at Kevin and Jeremy. At first, they had been hesitant about joining the other children. They worried aloud about their father and how Archy might be faring. But Maggie encouraged the boys to go outside, and they quickly forgot their father and joined the children. Maggie hoped that they could soon put all of their past behind them and enjoy being children.

"What are you thinking about?" Red asked, interrupting Maggie's thoughts.

"Their happiness," Maggie said, motioning toward the children.

Then her eyes slid over to the elderly chief's lodge. "And I wonder what's happening there," she confessed. "I feel for Wind Walker so much, for he is watching the old chief die."

"He is doing his duty to his chief," Red said, reaching a gentle hand to Maggie's cheek. "Soon, Maggie, Wind Walker will take the old chief's place. He will be chief."

"He will be a wonderful leader," Maggie said, nodding. She turned her gaze past the far edge of the village. "I wonder what is happening at Archy's ranch."

"I heard horses leaving the village last night

after you returned with the children," Red said, following her gaze.

"Yes, after thinking about it, Wind Walker thought it best to send scouts to keep an eye on Archy," Maggie explained. "I wonder what they found. They haven't returned yet."

"I hope they are safe," Red said, remembering the day of the ambush.

When he had fallen to the ground, wounded, he had thought he was living his last moments of life. Had Maggie and Wind Walker not arrived when they had, he believed he would have joined the others in the cold, dark ground.

He turned to Maggie. "My Magpie," he said, then brought one of her hands to his lips and kissed it.

"Red, I feel it, too." She bit her lip. "I know what you were thinking. You almost died, Red. Because of that evil man, you almost died. And so many of our friends are now gone."

"I only hope that those we sent ahead are alive and well," Red said. "When I am well enough to travel, I hope to go and find them."

"Maggie! Maggie!" Kevin yelled as he came running toward her. "Look at the bird egg! We found it beneath a tree!"

Maggie saw the tiny blue-speckled egg. It hadn't broken in the fall from its nest. "It's been there since spring just waiting for you to find it," she said, smiling at Kevin. "Most birds only lay eggs in the spring, but of course you know that."

"No, I didn't," Kevin said, his smile fading. "I hoped this was new and that I could help hatch the baby bird from it."

"No, it's not new," Maggie explained. "But you can keep the egg, anyway, for a keepsake."

"I will keep the egg safe in case the mother wants it again," Kevin said, gently cupping it in his hands.

"It's sweet of you to do that," Red said, reaching over and patting the young child on his frail shoulder. Red had quickly grown fond of the two young boys. But when one thought of how they had been treated by their father, who could not feel compassion for them?

Cradling the egg, Kevin smiled at Maggie and Red before running back to join the others.

"At least something good came of the tragedies," Maggie said, her voice breaking. "The children are safe. I hope Archy doesn't discover where they are."

"I must get off my feet," Red said, drawing Maggie's eyes back to him.

She saw the sweat on his brow and knew that was from the exertion. She took him gently by an elbow into Wind Walker's lodge.

She still couldn't believe that out here, in the middle of nowhere, where so many deaths and heartache had occurred, she had found happiness.

She knew that Wind Walker's heart was heavily burdened now with sadness. She wished she could go to him and help him, as he had helped her, but knew that time had to come later.

"Ah, look at those plush pelts," Red said, walking toward them where they lay beside the lodge fire.

"They are ermine and marten pelts," Maggie said, smiling when she saw her uncle's eyebrows raise at their worth.

"The Cheyenne have wealth in their own ways," Maggie said, helping her uncle down onto the pelts. "But mostly, their wealth is in their shared happiness."

"They are a fine people," Red said, sighing with relief when he was off his feet.

"The finest, and to think there are people who mock them and wish them dead," Maggie said, visibly shuddering.

"Yes, and always will," Red said, giving Maggie a troubled gaze. He knew that she would be a part of the Cheyenne forever. Her decision troubled him. The dangers of living with them were numerous.

His Sweet Magpie had chosen a life that might bring her more sorrow than happiness.

Chapter 29

I see thee better in the dark,
I do not need a light.
The love of thee a prism be
Excelling violet.
                —Emily Dickinson

With Chief Half Moon holding his own, Wind Walker had decided to proceed with his plan to get back at Archy.

Maggie rode with him and his warriors in the cover of darkness, the moon behind the clouds, lightning sending off its flashes once again far up in the mountains. For the first time since Maggie had begun to fear storms on the wagon train West, she was not afraid.

Suddenly, other hoofbeats were drumming across the land.

Wind Walker reached over and grabbed Maggie's reins, stopping her steed as he drew his own into a shuddering halt. The warriors stopped behind them.

Before they had the chance to find protective

cover, Wind Walker heard a low whistle, the sort the scouts from his clan used to warn others that they were near. The scouts that Wind Walker had sent out to observe Archy were returning with news about him.

Wind Walker gave a low whistle back and four men came out from the shadows.

"It is good to see you, Black Hawk," Wind Walker said, reaching over and placing a firm hand on the warrior's bare shoulder. "What do you have to report about Archibald Parrish?"

"He rides alone toward the mountains," Black Hawk said as Wind Walker took his hand away. "We did not follow. We wanted to report what we saw to you first. What do you think his reason is for riding toward the mountains?"

"Perhaps he is headed toward the Ute renegades stronghold," Wind Walker answered.

"And I have something else to report that you will find interesting," Black Hawk said, smiling slowly.

"What is that?" Wind Walker asked, forking an eyebrow.

"There is now only a small portion of men that remain loyal to Archy," Black Hawk said, his eyes gleaming. "It seems that many have abandoned him. Archy's manpower has been cut to less than half what it was."

"You are referring to those you saw left at the ranch since the stampede," Wind Walker said, looking past Black Hawk in the direction of Archy's ranch. "I had wondered why so few were helping him round up the animals. It must mean that they were gone before we came."

"It does seem so," Black Hawk said, nodding.

"So when we go to the ranch to start another stampede, there are only a few cowhands left to try and stop us," Wind Walker said. "They will regret having not left with the others, for I have plans for them."

Maggie sidled her horse over closer to Wind Walker's. "What are you going to do?" she asked, her eyes searching his. "Is it different than what you originally planned?"

"What I am going to do is something much easier on the cowhands than what Archy might do to them once he discovers that the rest of his longhorn are gone when he returns to his ranch," Wind Walker answered.

"Like what?" Maggie asked, her eyes wide.

"You shall see," Wind Walker said. "Just remember that many of those cowhands played a role in what happened to your friends. They deserve to have a part in the comeuppance, as well."

Wind Walker turned to Black Hawk again. "Go find Archy and follow him to wherever he might be going. Assume that he is headed for the Ute stronghold."

Black Hawk nodded, reached over and gave Wind Walker a fierce hug, then rode away again into the darkness of night with the other three scouts.

"Let us move onward, ourselves," Wind Walker said, looking over his shoulder at the other warriors. "Be careful. Let no harm come to you. The important thing is to stampede the rest of the longhorns. Then we will round up the cowhands that have stayed loyal to Archy and deal with them, as well. They should be gone when Archy returns."

"But he will have his Ute friends," Maggie said.

"I doubt for long," Wind Walker said. "If the Ute are smart, they will break their alliance with Archy. He is trouble for anyone."

"But we mustn't ever forget the Ute's role in what happened to my friends," Maggie said.

"Their comeuppance will come, too," Wind Walker said, giving Maggie an encouraging smile. "Their time as renegades is almost over."

Maggie returned the smile as they continued riding onward. She was so proud of Wind Walker, his convictions and his strengths.

They rode in the pitch black onward, until they finally heard the bellowing of longhorns that were somewhere close by. They heard snorting and more bellowing.

The moon slid from behind the clouds, revealing most of the cattle mingling close by, amidst thick, purple alfalfa plants. They blew off steam when the wind brought the smells of the horses and those who rode them.

"Make certain none are left this time!" Wind Walker shouted, joining those who were scattering the herd. Maggie stayed close at his side on her own steed, helping to scatter the huge animals by shouting and riding after them.

Wind Walker waited for retaliation. Archy's cowhands had surely heard the commotion, yet they did not come to interfere. Either they were gone, or they just did not care. Perhaps they were abandoning Archy, as the others had. It did seem that no one had any love for the cattle baron.

Suddenly, out of the darkness several cowhands appeared on horseback with rifles in hand. They were quickly surrounded. They dropped their firearms before they got one shot fired off, and cowered as Wind Walker and Maggie rode up to them.

"You know what to do!" he shouted at the warriors who quickly leaped from their horses. They rushed to the cowhands, who had slid from their saddles, and stood trembling beside their steeds.

Soon the cowhands were tied and gagged, their eyes wide with fear over the gags.

"Now what are you going to do with them?" Maggie asked.

"My brethren, you will take these men away from this place, in the opposite direction from where Archy was seen traveling," Wind Walker shouted. "When you get them far enough away, stop. Leave them without clothes, boots, and weapons. They then can decide where to go, whether it's back to the ranch, or to a fort where they can seek help and hope they won't have to pay for any of Archy's crimes. Or their own if they were a part of the ambush."

Maggie saw some of the men flinch, which seemed to prove they had been a part of the ambush. She felt no sympathy for them. She felt nothing. She only wanted them out of her sight, for looking at them reminded her of how many of those she loved were now in their graves.

Wind Walker looked over the cowhands, then nodded at a couple of his men. "I feel that this is not the last of them," he said. "Come with me. I want to check the bunkhouse and the main house."

Then he looked at Maggie. "Thus far tonight I have been able to keep you safe, but the closer we get to the ranch house, the worse the danger becomes. If anyone is left at the ranch, they will shoot to kill in hopes of saving their own hides."

He gazed intensely into the eyes of one of the cowhands. He leaned down and yanked the gag from his mouth. "Tell me how many are still there," he said firmly.

"Only one as far as I know," the man gulped out. "Cookie. The cook. He's been sleeping in the house, not the bunkhouse. I didn't see him leave tonight."

"Cookie!" Maggie gasped, recalling the obese, greasy-headed man who had taken care of the children after their mother died.

"Cookie?" Wind Walker asked, forking an eyebrow.

"I met him while I was imprisoned at the house," Maggie explained. "As far as I know, he's not the sort that would kill anyone. I never saw him with any weapons. He is a gentle sort, who does more womanly chores."

"That's right," the cowhand said. "That's exactly how he is. You've got nothing to fear from him. When he sees you all a'comin' toward the house, he'll either hightail it out the back door in an attempt to get away, or come out of the house, hands in the air, too cowardly to do anything else."

"You have been very cooperative in telling me these things," Wind Walker said, studying the lean man, whose dark eyes and long dark hair matched his.

He looked him slowly up and down, then peered intensely at his face.

"Where are you from?" Wind Walker asked. "What is your relationship with Archy? Did you stay with him because you wanted to, or because you were afraid to try to leave?"

"I am a breed," the man said, swallowing hard. "I came with Archy from Texas where my folks are from. My father was white. My mother is Apache."

"Why did you join forces with the likes of Archibald Parrish?" Maggie asked, realizing that man's confession seemed to affect Wind Walker. She could tell that he was torn now that he knew that he was part Indian.

"Money," the young man said. "Isn't that why most do what they do? I had no other way of makin' a livin'. I planned to take a pocketful of coins home to my mother. My father died long ago. He was shot in cold blood on the streets of Dallas. Since then, I was the man of the house. My mother awaits my return anxiously."

"And did Archy pay you well enough?" Wind Walker asked coldly. "Or did he cheat you?"

"I've enough, I guess," the young man said. "But that doesn't matter now, does it? You're going to take it all away from me by sending me out with the others and leaving me for the wolves, or whatever else is out there waiting."

"Did you ride with Archy on the day of my friends' ambush at the wagon train?" Maggie questioned. "Or did you stay behind that day and take care of the cattle?"

"I had no part in what happened that day at the camp," the young man said, shaking his head. "I only tend to cattle, ma'am. Nothing else. I didn't come out here to murder. I came to make coins to take home to my mother."

Maggie turned to Wind Walker. "Please let him go," she pleaded. "He's innocent. He's just been trapped in a life that turned sour probably the day he was born. You . . . you . . . know how breeds are looked upon in the white community. He's lucky he hasn't been shot."

Wind Walker gazed at length at the young man. "What is your name?"

"Charlie Three Clouds," the young man said. "But to keep from getting spit upon, I go by the name Charlie."

"Well, then, Charlie, come with me to the ranch house," Wind Walker said, nodding to a warrior to untie him. "I think there will be something there for you."

"You'll let me go?" Charlie gulped out. "What are you going to give me?"

Maggie questioned Wind Walker with her eyes, but didn't say anything.

"You will see," Wind Walker said.

He nodded toward Charlie's horse. "Mount your steed," he said. "Come with me and Maggie."

Charlie scurried to his horse and hurried into his saddle. He waited for Wind Walker to talk with his warriors, then rode between him and Maggie toward the ranch house.

"Do you think Cookie will come out as soon as he sees us, or run from the back of the house and hide?" Maggie asked, looking over at Charlie.

"I imagine he left the minute he heard the longhorns stampeding," Charlie said somberly. "I imagine he's running as hard as those pudgy old legs will carry him, as far as he can get from the house."

"Then we will let him go. I will not interfere," Wind Walker said tightly. "I will allow his escape."

They rode on up to the house that stood in silence. No lamplight glowed from any of the windows. The house looked like a huge black snake in the night as it rambled on to the right and left in its vastness.

"Maggie, Charlie, come with me," Wind Walker said, drawing a tight rein in front of the house.

He dismounted, grabbed his rifle from its gunboot, then moved cautiously up the steps as Maggie and Charlie silently followed. When they got inside without anyone there to stop them, Wind Walker gazed over at Maggie.

"Find a lamp," he said. "Light it."

She nodded.

Soon she was carrying a kerosene lamp from room to room with Wind Walker and Charlie, stopping when Wind Walker stepped into what appeared to be Archy's study.

Without any thought, Wind Walker went to what he knew was a white man's safe, where all valuables and money were known to be stored. He found it halfway open. He smiled and opened the door the rest of the way, reached in, and grabbed two heavy bags. He turned to Charlie and tossed them both at him.

"What are you doing?" Charlie paled as he caught the bag of coins. "What do you want me to do with these?"

"You worked hard for those coins," Wind Walker said, grabbing more from the safe. "They are now yours."

After loading down the man's arms with more bags of coins, Wind Walker gestured with a hand toward the door. "You can go now. Do not stop until you are safely away from Wyoming land. Hurry to your mother. Give her this Cheyenne warrior's blessing."

Maggie was touched by Wind Walker's act of humanity, making everything else that he had done seem like nothing. His heart had gone out to this young man and his sad story. He was giving help where help was needed. He trusted the young man to do the right thing with the coins that had been handed him.

Maggie went to Charlie. "Don't let Wind Walker down by doing anything but giving your mother the money," she said softly. "I know how tempting it could be to have so much money when you've never had any before. Take it home. Give it to your mother. Your reward will be the look in her eyes."

"I won't let you or Wind Walker down," Charlie said, tears rushing from his eyes. "I promise with all of my heart that I will take this to my mother. I could never do anything else with it. She deserves some good in her life. Thank you, Wind Walker, for giving it to her."

"It will be your gift to her, not mine," Wind Walker said, placing a gentle hand on the young man's lean shoulder. "You worked hard for it. You worked under the worst of circumstances. Go now. Be careful. Let no one steal this from you. May *Maheo* be with you all of the way."

"Thank you. Thank you," Charlie said, unable to hug Wind Walker, his hands and arms so full with bags of coins. He smiled through his tears over at Maggie. "And thank you. I wish you well."

He hurried from the room.

Maggie went to Wind Walker and hugged him. "You never cease to amaze me."

"When I see injustice, I try to right it whenever possible," he said honestly.

The sound of footsteps in the corridor coming toward the study made Maggie and Wind Walker turn quickly. Her mouth dropped open at the sight of Cookie.

He stopped just inside the door, his head hung humbly.

"Have mercy on me," he choked out, his eyes moving slowly up from Maggie to Wind Walker. "I've never been a part of Archy's schemes, except to be his friend. I never rode with him nor did any killin'. As you can see by my size, I'm not the sort who fits on a horse very well. I've just been his cook and whatever else he needs me for in his house. I apologize for the wrong he's done, but other than that, there ain't nothing else I can do 'bout it."

Maggie turned to Wind Walker. "I believe him. He took care of the children the best way he knew how when their mother died. He was the cook for all of the cowhands."

"I was the main cook," Cookie said, his eyes pleading. "Even when Sarah was alive, I did most of the cooking. She wasn't all that knowledgeable about food and the like. When Archy married her, she was a dancehall queen. Those sorts of women ain't been taught much about cooking. I . . . I . . . believe that's why she couldn't live under the pressures of the ranch. Little by little she died inside. I saw it as God's grace when she went on to her reward. She was miserable. Just miserable."

"What would you like to do?" Wind Walker asked. "Where would you like to go? I do not hold you guilty for what Archy has done."

Cookie looked sheepishly over at Maggie, then at Wind Walker. "I'd like to be taken to where the kids are," he said, his voice breaking. "I've grown fond of them. I . . . I . . . miss them."

"They might be staying at the Indian village with me and Wind Walker," Maggie said softly. "They don't have anyone else to go to. I have grown fond of them, too. I wouldn't mind taking care of them."

"Then . . . can . . . I stay with them . . . with you?" Cookie asked, begging with his eyes. "I can cook. I can clean."

Maggie laughed softly, then turned to Wind Walker. "What do you think?" she asked, her eyes searching his.

"I was not planning on taking anyone back to the village with us," he said. He gazed intensely into Cookie's eyes. "Do you truly wish to be a part of the Cheyenne life?"

"If I can be," Cookie replied. "I ain't never been that happy anywheres else. I just want to be with the children. They are all the family I've had for years. As for Archy? I saw doom coming his way long ago. No one could do the sorts of things he did and live for long."

"You are welcome to come, if you wish," Wind Walker said, then took Maggie by the hand. "It is time to go home."

Cookie gazed at Wind Walker again. "Like I said, I never fit well onto a horse," he said, swallowing hard. "Can I take a wagon to your village? That's the only way I can travel anywhere."

"Yes, get your belongings. Go for the wagon," Wind Walker said, walking from the room with Maggie. "We will wait for you."

They went on outside.

"Your heart is bigger than the beautiful moon in the sky," she said, moving into his embrace. "If only the entire world could know your goodness. If only there were more like you."

He held her to him, thinking the same about her, for never in his life had he known a woman of such compassion. Soon all of this would be behind them and they could have a wonderful life. Their hearts would become as one. They would speak vows that would seal their love forever.

But there were still some obstacles in the way. Especially the sadness that would come the day he had to bury the ailing *sachem,* Half Moon.

He had felt free enough to leave tonight to finish this mission. But what of tomorrow? Would that be the day that his chief would take his last breath and start his journey to the stars?

He watched Cookie amble from the house and head toward the barn. He led a harnessed team of sleepy-eyed horses with a creaky wagon out into the night.

"There is one thing left to do to make certain Archy feels his losses deeply," Wind Walker said to Maggie.

"What is that?"

"Watch," Wind Walker said. He went to Cookie. "Get what animals you want and tie them to your wagon."

"Animals?" Cookie said, his eyebrows arched.

His gaze followed Wind Walker's and saw that he was looking at the two cows that were in their own private fence.

He looked at Wind Walker again. "Those animals?"

"Yes, and what else is in the barn that you would like to take," Wind Walker said. "It is now yours."

"Horses?" Cookie said, his eyes wide. "There are three left besides the two I have here."

"Get them," Wind Walker said dryly. "Quickly."

Maggie was puzzled by what Wind Walker was doing. She stood back and watched Cookie get the two cows, and then the horses, tying them with a rope to the back of the wagon.

Then she went pale as Wind Walker made a torch from straw he took from the barn.

"Maggie," Wind Walker said over his shoulder as he handed the torch to one of his warriors. "Get the lamp I saw hanging in the barn. Light it."

She gave him a quiet look. She no longer needed to guess what he was going to do. He was going to make sure Archy came home to *nothing*.

She went and got the lamp that hung just inside the barn door. She found matches on a nearby shelf. She soon had a flame started on the wick of the lamp and handed the lamp over to Wind Walker.

She went and stood with Cookie as Wind Walker lit more torches and passed them to his warriors. They tossed them onto the roof of the house, then the bunkhouse, and the other outbuildings, until the whole sky seemed to blaze.

"It is done," Wind Walker said. He turned to his warriors. "It is time to take the white men far away. You know what to do. Leave now."

They nodded and soon the cowhands had ropes tied around their necks, and were trailing behind the warriors' horses, on foot.

Wind Walker turned to Maggie. "Now it is time to go home," he said. He nodded to Cookie. "Come. You are welcome in my village."

Wind Walker and Maggie mounted their steeds and rode back in the direction of their village, with Cookie and his animals following behind them.

Chapter 30

It was the limit of my dream,
The focus of my prayer,—
A perfect, paralyzing bliss,
Contented as despair.
                    —Emily Dickinson

Feeling uncomfortable for the first time as he sat with Dark Arrow and the others, Archy felt that the tension might snap at any moment. He sat beside an outdoor fire high up in the mountains where Dark Arrow had successfully established himself a stronghold that no one had ever been able to find.

When he built his fires, the smoke mingled with the floating haze that always seemed present in this part of the mountains, making it invisible to the naked eye.

Because of their tight friendship, and firm in the knowledge that Archy would never dare tell the location under the threat of death, Dark Arrow had taken Archy to his stronghold many moons ago. But tonight, as the clouds continued to tease the moon, covering it, then uncovering it again, Archy did not have that same feeling of camaraderie that he had always felt with Dark Arrow.

He could only gather that the reason for Dark Arrow's aloofness might be that Archy had come and asked for one favor too many.

At this very moment, the slim, muscled leader was squinting untrusting eyes at Archy.

Archy could feel the cold stares of the rest of the men as they sat around the fire. Some of them were eating meat that had been cooking slowly over the fire for many hours, while others smoked their long-stemmed pipes. They usually accepted Archy with open arms, each warrior generous with a plate of food or a shared smoke. But tonight, they were lacking in friendship. There was a coldness among the renegades.

"What's up?" he asked nervously. "Why am I getting the cold shoulder? Haven't I always been truthful with you?"

He glanced over his shoulder at the pile of stolen property that had been brought to the stronghold, yet strangely enough hardly ever touched or used by any of the renegades. It was the plundering that brought them excitement, not the plunder itself.

His gaze locked on a toy baby carriage with a limp rag doll hanging over its one side. The carriage had to have been stolen from a wagon train. Archy wondered what happened to the child it belonged to.

"Your reason for being here is not a good one," Dark Arrow finally said, interrupting Archy's troubled thoughts.

Archy suddenly felt a strong sense of guilt that he had never felt before. He had never actually witnessed any children being killed on the raids, yet knew there must have been, for they were always with the adults who were seeking a new life in the West.

"What do you mean . . . not a good one?" Archy pushed down his feelings. "You've never hesitated before when I came to you askin' for your assistance. What is the difference tonight?"

Dark Arrow leaned forward, the reflection of the fire in his eyes glowing red. "What is the difference?" he said, his lips pulling into a menacing, taunting smile. "*I* will gain nothing from it. That is the difference."

"What do you want as payment for helping me find my sons and the ones who are responsible for stampeding my herd?" Archy asked, his spine stiffening as Dark Arrow continued to glare at him. "Tell me. It will be yours."

"Everything," Dark Arrow said, snickering. "Everything you possess. Give it to me and I will give you the names of those who caused the stampede and stole your sons."

Archy paled. "Everything? Lord, Dark Arrow, you know that I can't do that. Why would you even expect me to? You've been my friend for a long time. Why are you taking advantage of that friendship now by making such asinine demands of me?"

"Asinine?" Dark Arrow said, angered that the word was being used to describe him. "You say that word as though you label *me* asinine. Is that what you meant to do?"

Archy realized his error. "Lord, no. I . . . I . . . was wrong to use that word. That's not what I meant to say."

"Because you truly feel that way," Dark Arrow said. He chuckled. "But that is all right. I forgive you."

Archy felt relief flood him. "Thank you. You were only joshing me, weren't you, when you said I had to give you all that I possess in order to get your help?"

"*Gah-ween*, no, I was not playing a game with you," Dark Arrow said, shrugging. "I always mean what I say. I will give you the information you seek if you promise to hand over all that you possess."

Archy leaned closer to the fire, looking directly into Dark Arrow's eyes. "You are acting as though you know where my sons are now, without searching for them. Is that true? Or did I misread what you said?"

"You read me right," Dark Arrow said. "I know exactly where your sons are, and who took them." He laughed cynically. "I know who caused your stampede."

"You do?" Archy said incredulously. "How could you?"

"How could I know more than you about these things?" Dark Arrow said, his eyes now two slits as he stared intensely over the fire at Archy. "Why? Because you are a stupid man and I am clever."

Archy's eyes filled with anger. He had to force himself not to jump over the fire and place his hands around the throat of the thieving, murdering renegade. But now was not the time to even think such a thing. He would be dead instantly if he so much as tried.

He decided to go ahead and play this game with the renegade leader, especially if it would finally gain him the knowledge that he sought. And to hell with agreeing to give up all that he owned. Once he got the information he needed, just let the renegades come and try to get what was his. He'd be waiting with the rest of his cowhands, the rifles aimed and ready for the bellies of each of these heartless, murdering thieves.

"I call you stupid because your brain is the

size of a pebble one can pluck from a riverbed,"
Dark Arrow said. Again he laughed cynically.
"*Ay-uh,* that is your brain, Archibald Parrish."

"Why would you say that?" Archy asked between gritted teeth, his hands doubled into
tight fists where they rested on his lap.

"Because you do not know where your children are and I do," Dark Arrow said, idly
shrugging. "You do not know where the white
woman with the red hair is. I do."

Archy lurched to his feet. "You know all of
that, and you play a game with me? I want my
sons. I want Maggie back. I want vengeance on
those who stole them and caused the stampede. And you just sit there and mock me?"

"*Ay-uh,* I know," Dark Arrow said, standing
so his eyes were even with Archy's.

"Tell me, damn it," Archy shouted. "Tell me
now. I'm wasting time. I need to go and get
what is mine. I want my sons. I want Maggie!"

"I know you well, Archibald Parrish, and
getting your sons and the woman is the last
thing that is on your mind," Dark Arrow said.
He walked slowly around the fire toward
Archy. "You think more of the longhorns than
you do your children. You want the woman
back only because she was a possession stolen
from you. You want the name of the man who
took all of this from you, yet the vengeance you
seek is for your lost longhorns."

He reached Archy. He stood directly in front of him, his eyes dancing with amusement.

"Am I right?" Dark Arrow asked. "Or am I wrong?"

"What difference does it make?" Archy said, his teeth clenched, his heart pounding. "Why would you even care? Tell me, Dark Arrow. Tell me! Come with me and join my vengeance. We work well together."

"We *worked* well together," Dark Arrow said tightly.

"What do you mean . . . worked?" Archy asked, searching the renegade's eyes. "Why do you use the past tense?"

"I do not want to ride with you ever again, especially against the likes of Wind Walker's warriors," Dark Arrow said. "You are not worth the risk. You are on your own now. Get out and do not show your face here again."

He pointed toward the mountain pass that led downward away from his stronghold.

"Go. Go now," he said flatly. "Never come here again or I will plant you in the ground. Alive."

Archy felt the color drain from his face, as he stumbled backward.

"You . . . you mentioned Wind Walker," Archy said, his pulse racing.

"Because he is the one who has outwitted you," Dark Arrow said. He stared directly into

Archy's pale blue eyes. "If you seek vengeance against him, he will be the victor. He is a clever man.

"He is good, I am bad. He has his life. I have mine." Dark Arrow shrugged, then laughed. "Mine is much more exciting than his."

Archy glared at Dark Arrow as he digested what he had been told. Wind Walker! That damn Cheyenne warrior who would one day be a powerful chief.

Not if I can help it, he swore to himself.

Dark Arrow suddenly yanked a knife from the sheath at his right side. He held it close to Archy's throat.

"Do you see this knife?" Dark Arrow said in a sneer.

"Yes, and I think I feel it, it's so damn close to my neck," Archy said. "Damn it, Dark Arrow. Are you planning on killing me? Do you hate me that much? What did I do to deserve your wrath?"

"Exist," Dark Arrow said. Then he took the knife away and threw his head back in a throaty laugh.

Archy breathed hard as he rubbed his neck. He watched Dark Arrow, realizing that he was in the presence of a madman. He started to wonder if Dark Arrow was going to allow him to leave.

Dark Arrow motioned with the knife toward

the pass. "I will give you one last chance. If you do not leave now, you will be responsible for your own death," he threatened.

"I'm going," Archy said, sliding past Dark Arrow. "I'm going."

He hurried to his horse and mounted it. Without looking back, he started to make his way down the tiny mountain pass, his heart racing, his eyes watching all around him.

He could hear movement in the brush at his left side. His throat went dry. Dark Arrow could have sent one of his renegades to follow him.

Or it might be a panther.

He was not going to allow himself to fear the unknown. He was lucky to have been able to leave the renegades' camp. He was never so afraid than he was at the moment he realized he was no longer Dark Arrow's friend. He had begun to count the last minutes of his life.

When the pass grew broader and less dangerous, Archy rode faster, relieved when he no longer heard movement around him.

"Wind Walker," he whispered, feeling free now to concentrate on something else besides keeping his hide intact.

He had thought about Wind Walker possibly being responsible for Maggie's abduction, but the rest? No. He had not thought that Wind Walker was capable of it. He was a man of peace. He had never given Archy any cause to fear him.

"Maggie?" he whispered, his eyebrows raising at the thought of Wind Walker coming for her in the night.

Yes, he could understand why Wind Walker would do that. Who wouldn't want her? He could even now smell the sweetness of her skin and see her beautiful face in his mind's eye.

He knew that he could not get back at Wind Walker as he wished to. He had only half the manpower he once had. He certainly didn't have enough men to take on the Cheyenne.

He would have to think of a better way to get back at Wind Walker and at the same time get Maggie and his sons into his possession again.

He rode onward, knowing that to stop and rest now, far away from the ranch, might be tempting fate just too much.

As long as he was moving, he was safe.

He did not have that much farther to go. If it were daylight, he would be able to see his ranch from this distance, but the moon was gone again. Everything around him was still in the darkness.

Suddenly he saw something flickering in the distance.

"Fire!" he said, his voice breaking, for he had no doubt what was burning. "My ranch!"

Now on level ground, he sank his heels into the flanks of his horse. He rode hard until he came to where smoke was so thick it choked him. He kept onward.

Morning started to break along the horizon, and there was enough light for him to see what lay ahead of him.

His ranch house was almost burned to the ground. His outbuildings were gone!

Then something else came to him. There were no longhorns! They were gone!

He looked at the ruins of the bunkhouse again. The men were gone.

Where was Cookie?

He dismounted his horse. He fell to his knees, a beaten man. Then slowly anger replaced hopelessness. He was all alone in the world now and all but penniless. He must make the one he knew was responsible pay!

"Wind Walker," he shouted to the heavens. "Damn you, Wind Walker!"

He rose again and mounted his horse. He rode onward even though there was nothing left to ride to.

The Cheyenne. Maggie. They were allies in this crime. And why would Wind Walker do all of these things? Why?

Her.

Chapter 31

Look back on time with kindly eyes,
He doubtless did his best;
How softly sinks his trembling sun,
In human nature's west!
    —Emily Dickinson

Maggie lay on a pallet of furs beside the lodge fire in Wind Walker's, and now her tepee. She became lost in thought as she watched the flames caressing the logs.

One full week had passed since she had watched Archibald Parrish's house burn. No one had seen or heard from him since.

The scouts hadn't found any trace of him when they had searched for him on the night of the house fire. It was hard for Maggie to believe that Archy had taken defeat this easily, yet it seemed he had. Maggie hoped he went back to Texas.

Cookie had said that was where he had met Archy all those years ago. They had become good friends, but as the years passed Cookie had seen Archy's greed worsen. He had thought about leaving Archy more than once. But the children were what had kept Cookie from going. He had been concerned about them even when their mother was alive. They had never had the sort of attention from her as they should. But she had seen that they were at least fed and bathed.

Now away from Archy, Cookie had joined Red and the two children in Red's tepee. The two grown-ups had become instant friends. And Red had grown quickly fond of the children.

Red, Cookie, and the children had decided to move on together as soon as Red was well enough to travel.

Maggie moved to her knees and stirred the stew that was simmering in a huge pot that hung from a tripod right over the flames of the fire. She was learning quickly how to cook many things that she now knew were Wind Walker's favorites.

She went with the other women to gather herbs, wild greens, and other varied roots that helped season the stews and soups. She had several stored for the winter that was close at hand now. The autumn leaves were falling steadily from the trees, resembling colored rain as they fell from their limbs.

It still seemed strange to her that she was actually there to stay and that she was a wife to a man she would always adore. Yes, she was married.

Wind Walker was hers forever.

She gazed toward the closed entrance flap, wondering how things were going for Wind Walker as he made his evening visit to his fallen chief's grave. She admired Wind Walker so much, in that even in death he gave the old chief respect and love.

So much had happened in the past week.

Wind Walker had seen her uneasiness in sleeping with him while unwed, her uncle just a few feet away in his own tepee. Maggie had worried about how it looked to her uncle for her to be with Wind Walker not only through the day, but also all night. She had always been a moral, God-loving person who attended church every Sunday in Boston. So, Wind Walker had hurried their wedding ceremony.

It was a brief, yet sweet ceremony. They had sealed their love with words of forever. She hoped even now to have a child growing in her womb.

Of course she knew that as anxious as her uncle was to move on, hoping to catch up with the others, he would never see or hold her child. But just to be able to tell him that she was with child would mean a lot to her, and him. He knew that she had always adored children and hoped to have some of her own when she married.

But she also knew that he was almost well enough to travel. If he just held on for another couple of weeks, she might have news to share with him. She had already missed her monthly.

She gazed at the entrance flap again. It was taking Wind Walker longer than usual to say his nightly prayers over the old chief's grave. It just seemed so hard for Wind Walker to accept that the chief was gone. He had died four nights ago.

The whole village was in mourning, yet took the time to see that Wind Walker was handed the title of chief in a brief, yet tender ceremony.

There was pride in having a new, young, vital chief. He was a man they all had counted on to help keep them safe even before their elderly chief had taken his last breath. In a sense, Wind Walker had been their chief for some time now. For so long now, he had made all of the decisions.

Maggie yawned and stretched her arms over her head. She was strangely tired these days, which might be a symptom of pregnancy. She snuggled against the pelts.

She turned to her side and again watched the fire, her stomach rumbling and growling with hunger.

She was beginning to be concerned about

Wind Walker. He had never taken this much time at his chief's grave.

She felt her body relaxing. Slowly her eyes closed. She smiled as she drifted off into a sweet, serene sleep, already dreaming about Wind Walker.

Then a sudden sound jolted Maggie from her sleep. It was a strange sound that was close, very close behind her. . . .

Her eyes quickly flew open, very aware that the sound was real, and not something that had happened in her dream.

A knife was slicing through the buckskin covering at the back of the tepee. Her heart pounded as though many drums were inside her chest.

Maggie turned and gasped. The tip of a knife and the hand that held it were poking through the slit. She saw the shadow of a man as it fell within the tepee after his other hand lifted the cut buckskin.

For a moment Maggie did not dare to breathe or stir.

Archy stepped through the long slit in the buckskin hide. Maggie leaped to her feet and took a quick step away from him.

"Well, hello, Maggie," Archy said, laughing throatily.

She saw how disheveled his clothes were. They were dirty and she could smell him clear across the tepee. His hair was even more greasy and stringy than before. His face had a week's growth of hair on it.

"Stay away from me," Maggie said breathlessly.

Her mind was swirling a mile a minute with what to do to protect herself against this demon. If she didn't act now, she might not be alive long enough to see her husband again.

"You know you're glad to see me," Archy said, still standing just inside the tepee, the knife held out threateningly before him.

Something clicked in Maggie's mind, something that Wind Walker had told her one day as she prepared their supper. He had told her about a woman who accidentally overturned soup into the fire. He was trying to warn Maggie to be careful of the larger pots filled with hot liquid.

Well, tonight, she was not cooking soup, but the stew had enough liquid in it to do the trick!

She reached over quickly and tipped the pot so that the leftover stew poured down into the flames of the fire. Just as she hoped it would do, it made a sound like an explosion. Ashes and steam flew up through the smoke hole at the top.

Archy was stunned for a moment by the sound. But he recovered quickly and started to rush Maggie to grab her. Suddenly Wind

Walker was there, his entrance so swift even Maggie was dazed by it.

"Maggie, step aside," Wind Walker said sternly. "Now!"

Maggie ran to the farthest side of the tepee, away from Archy.

"Come ahead," Archy said, brandishing his weapon menacingly before him.

Wind Walker grabbed his own knife from its sheath at his side. The men stood facing each other, slowly moving their knives in the air, then making a lunge for each other.

Maggie screamed as a scuffle ensued, the knife blades glinting in the fire's glow. Wind Walker rolled over to one side. Archy followed.

Wind Walker dropped his knife and grabbed Archy's wrist. The knife was close to Wind Walker's face. Maggie waited for the death plunge that would take her husband from her.

Then suddenly Archy was on the bottom and Wind Walker had the knife taken from the evil man. Again there was a standoff as Archy held Wind Walker's wrist, the knife now only a fraction from Archy's throat. Suddenly Archy's hand slipped away from Wind Walker's. The knife made a downward plunge, but only getting Archy in the shoulder, Wind Walker purposely changing the course of the knife.

Archy let out a loud, painful scream as Wind

Walker took the knife from the wound. Archy reached for his bleeding shoulder, then went silent when his two sons ran into the tepee and saw him.

"Pa?" Jeremy said, his eyes wide.

"Pa?" Kevin gulped out.

"Yes, it's your father," Maggie said, as she went to them and gathered them into her arms. "He's all right. It's only a slight wound."

They seemed afraid to go to Archy.

Red came into the tepee. He gazed in disbelief at Archy.

"Well, now ain't this one happy family?" Archy said sarcastically as he moved to his feet, his one hand on his wound, blood seeping through his fingers. He glared from one to the other.

"You were all in on it, weren't you?" he said, his voice drawn. "You all took everything away from me."

Cookie came into the tepee. Archy's face went ashen when he saw him.

"You?" Archy gulped out. "You were a part of this? You wanted to see me lose everything?"

"Archy, you lost at life long ago," Cookie said, his voice quivering. "Sorry, ol' pal. Sorry as hell you had to turn out the way you did. You just had to have too much, didn't you?"

"And I did until . . . until . . . I went to that

damn wagon train and saw a redheaded woman," Archy said, his eyes flashing into Maggie's. "It's all because of you, you witch."

"You have said enough." Wind Walker grabbed Archy by an elbow.

"What're you gonna do with me?" Archy asked.

"Tonight your wound will be seen to. Then tomorrow you will be taken to Fort Bent," Wind Walker said dryly. "I will let Colonel Braddock decide what your final fate will be."

"No." Archy shook his head vehemently. "He's the kind who likes to place a noose around a man's neck. I'll hang for sure."

His eyes went to his children. "Boys, you won't let that happen to your pa, now, will you?"

When they said nothing back to him, he looked at Cookie again. "You won't let your ol' pal die in such a way, will you?"

Cookie didn't respond. Archy hung his head and walked from the tepee with Wind Walker. The children began crying as they clung to Maggie.

"Will he hang?" they sobbed.

"I'm not sure what will become of your father," Maggie answered honestly. "But you know as well as I that he deserves to be punished."

"I'll bring the boys back to my tepee," Red

said, taking them both by a hand. He smiled at Maggie. "It's over, hon. Now you can have that family with the man you love without always having to worry about Archy Parrish interfering."

"Red, how did you know that I . . . that I think I might be pregnant?" Maggie asked with a smile.

"Maggie, I know you even better than you know yourself," Red said, chuckling. "All I have to do is look in your eyes to know that something is happening inside you. There is a radiance about you. I hear that being pregnant can cause that."

Maggie laughed. She went to Red and gave him a hug, then watched him leave with the children.

Wind Walker came back to the tepee a short time later.

"Where did you take Archy?" Maggie asked.

"I took him to Sky Dreamer to see to the wound. Then I tied him up out by the fire," Wind Walker said, drawing her into his arms. "He will be safe enough. The night creatures do not come into our village. The fire keeps them away."

"I'll just feel better about things once he is totally out of our lives," she said softly.

Wind Walker's eyes were looking past her. She turned and followed his gaze and saw the bloodstains on the mats and pelts, then saw the huge split in the buckskin covering.

"Let us go and spend the rest of the night with Red and the boys," Wind Walker suggested. "Red will be leaving soon. I know you would like to have as much time as you can with him."

"Yes, I would," Maggie said, then smiled mischievously. "Wind Walker, do you see something different about me?"

Wind Walker placed gentle hands at her shoulders and looked into her eyes, then smiled. "I have seen it these past days, yes," he said. "You are beaming, my woman. It is more than that. There is a glow about you."

"Can you imagine why?" she teased.

"I might," Wind Walker said. He swept her fully into his arms. "You are with child."

"Do you truly believe so?" she asked, then smiled as he nodded and kissed her.

She, too, was almost positive she was with child. She could hardly wait to see if it was a boy or a girl, but either would be perfect. He or she would be an extension of her and Wind Walker's love.

Chapter 32

Beautiful was the night. Behind the black wall
   of the forest,
Tipping its summit with silver, arose the moon.
                    —Henry Wadsworth Longfellow

The fire's glow was soft as it burned in the firepit in Wind Walker and Maggie's tepee.

Wind Walker lay on his side on their blankets of rich pelts and furs, his eyes looking first at Maggie, who lay beside him, and then his son, who was nestled in Maggie's arms.

A short while ago, Maggie had gone with Wind Walker to the river and placed gifts on the old, charred tree for Wind Walker's first wife, Sweet Willow. This was a ritual that Maggie now shared with him, for she knew that he was still devoted to his first wife.

She felt no jealousy over anything in his past, only blessed that they would be together for an eternity.

"Dancing Wind," Maggie murmured as her

four-month-old son suckled from her milk-filled breast. "Isn't he the most beautiful baby, Wind Walker?"

"Yes, beautiful and perfect," he said, reaching to run a hand over his son's tiny head. He smiled as he felt the slight fuzz.

He was proud that Dancing Wind's coloring was the same as his, for he would one day be a valiant Cheyenne warrior, his dark hair long down his back, his copper face proud as he rode his steed. But his son's eyes, they were a reflection of his mother's—green as spring grass.

"We shall have a daughter next," Wind Walker said, reaching a gentle hand to his wife's lovely face. "What a beautiful maiden she will be."

"I do look forward to having a daughter," Maggie replied. "I never had a sister. I want that for Dancing Wind. I enjoyed having Uncle Patrick around, but it wasn't the same."

She smiled down at her son, thinking about how proud her uncle Patrick was of him, too. He came each day and gazed in wonder at him.

Red had not continued with the journey West to Oregon, after all. He had not been able to break the strong bond between himself and Maggie. Now one was growing stronger each day with Maggie's chieftain husband.

Red had taken over a portion of the land that

had once been claimed by Archibald Parrish. He had rebuilt part of the ranch house. He had even found and kept several of the longhorns and was watching them multiply as more were born.

Cookie had resumed his role of "mother" to Kevin and Jeremy, who were the happiest of children now. They were unofficially adopted by Red, and came often to play and hunt with the Cheyenne boys.

There was one thing more that made Maggie happy. Little Sparrow and Red were infatuated with each other. Maggie believed there would be a wedding soon. Then Kevin and Jeremy would have a true mother.

"I know you are very proud that you and your warriors tracked down and finally found the Ute renegades," she said.

"Yes, for a while I had to forget the peaceful side of me when I ended Dark Arrow's reign of terror," he said, nodding. "He and his renegade friends are no longer of this earth."

"And then there is Archibald Parrish," Maggie said. "He wasn't condemned to death, but instead he is behind bars for the rest of his life. Red took a lot of pleasure in telling him face-to-face that he had taken over Archy's ranch, and found several of his longhorns. I would have loved to have seen the look on Archy's face."

"Yes, he finally got his comeuppance," Wind Walker said, chuckling.

Maggie gazed down at her son. "Just look at him." She sighed as she slid Dancing Wind's lips from her breast. "He is not only content-edly full, but he is asleep."

She gently wrapped a soft pelt around their tiny son, leaving only his beautiful copper face exposed.

"I shall take him to his cradle," Wind Walker said, gently taking Dancing Wind from his wife's loving arms.

Maggie watched Wind Walker as he carried the baby to his cradle, laying him there, then lingering to watch Dancing Wind for another moment.

Maggie's contentment was so complete she was afraid that she might wake up and realize that all of this was just a beautiful dream. But when Wind Walker came back to her, knelt over her, and brought his lips down onto hers, she knew that no dream could ever be this wonderful. This was the real thing.

And they were ready to face another long winter together. Maggie had discovered quite quickly that winters were often terribly severe on the plains. The snow was deep, the wind howled, and the temperatures dropped so low, she knew that it had to have been below zero.

But she had learned how the terribly cold

days were spent in the Cheyenne village. The men spent their days repairing weapons and gear, and making such new items for their households as were needed. Women adorned hides, fashioned containers, cooked, tended the babies, and gossiped. The children did only the necessary chores and spent the rest of the time playing winter games and getting away with as much mischief as they could.

Maggie had spent her first winter just being with her husband and dreaming of the child she carried within her womb, as well as learning all that she could about being a Cheyenne.

She was proud to say that she was of the Golden Eagle Clan of *Shahiyena*, Cheyenne. She loved being in Wyoming country. There you sensed that you were somehow on the edge of the world.

Maggie twined her arms around Wind Walker as he stretched out over her, soon filling her with his wondrous heat, moving rhythmically within her.

Maggie trembled as she came alive with his deepened kiss. His thrusts within her seemed magical. They took her away into another world of passion.

When she was with him in this way, she experienced utter tenderness and complete joy. There was never any part of her body that did not tingle when her husband held her and kissed her. She was melting inside; her husband promised nothing but the enduring passion only he knew how to create.

Her head reeled as the pleasure mounted. She was overcome with such an unbearable sweetness as his lips moved downward to swirl his tongue around one nipple and then the other. And then he kissed her lips again, his hands moving over her, touching, caressing, loving.

She gave herself up to the wild ecstasy, the sensual abandonment, as she felt the glorious bliss rising and growing hotter within her.

Wind Walker's heart was pounding as he sculpted himself more closely to his wife's body. He pressed deeper within her, searching for that precious moment when they both exploded with passion.

He was aware of Maggie's gasps becoming long, soft whimpers. He felt the pleasure growing, spreading, then made one last deep thrust within her, their bodies jolting and quivering as they found complete ecstasy again within each other's arms.

Maggie clung to him. She returned his kiss with trembling lips.

She sucked in a wild breath of bliss as he stroked her womanhood, bringing her more pleasure.

She closed her eyes and sighed as he whispered against her lips how much he loved her. After a few minutes, he took her to the stars and beyond again as he entered her with his powerful manliness.

"I shall always love you," Wind Walker whispered against her lips.

"As I will always love you," Maggie whispered back.

Their eyes met and held.

They smiled at each other, then kissed again.

She remembered when they first met and she had thought that he was taking her as a captive, when in truth, he was rescuing her from a fate worse than death.

In a sense, though, she *had* been his captive from the moment they had looked into each other's eyes . . . a captive of his heart!

"My Wind Walker . . ." she whispered.

LETTER TO THE READER

Dear Reader:

I hope you enjoyed *Wind Walker*. The next book in my Signet Indian Series is *Proud Eagle*. It is about the very proud and noble Makah Indians of the Pacific Northwest. *Proud Eagle* is filled with excitement, romance, and adventure, and will be in the stores December 2004.

For those of you who are collecting my Indian romances, my entire backlist of books and information about how to acquire them can be found online at www.cassieedwards.com. If you would like information about my fan club, you can send for my latest newsletter, bookmark, and my autographed photograph at:

CASSIE EDWARDS
6709 North Country Club Road
Mattoon, IL 61938

For an assured, prompt reply, please send a stamped self-addressed legal-sized envelope.

Thank you for your support of my Indian series. I love researching and writing about our country's Native Americans, the very first, true people of our proud land.

Cassie Edwards